Warwickshire County Council

8/16			LL
28/5/16*			

This item is to be returned or renewed before the latest date above. It may be borrowed for a further period if not in demand. **To renew your books:**

- **Phone the 24/7 Renewal Line 01926 499273 or**
- **Visit www.warwickshire.gov.uk/libraries**

Discover • Imagine • Learn • *with libraries*

BIG GIRLS DON'T CRY

It is 1962, and WPC Bobbie Blandford is in her third year at Stony End station. Her relationship with boyfriend Dr Leo Stanhope is decidedly rocky, and she faces a continuing struggle to earn the same respect that is paid to her male colleagues. When a violent bank robbery shocks the entire village, Bobbie's talented — but seemingly troubled — brother Tom arrives from Scotland Yard, placing her on the sidelines of the investigation. Can Bobbie find out the truth, resolve things with Leo, and stop her brother from ruining his career?

Books by Sally Quilford
in the Linford Romance Library:

THE SECRET OF HELENA'S BAY
BELLA'S VINEYARD
A COLLECTOR OF HEARTS
MY TRUE COMPANION
AN IMITATION OF LOVE
SUNLIT SECRETS
MISTLETOE MYSTERY
OUR DAY WILL COME
BONFIRE MEMORIES
MIDNIGHT TRAIN
TAKE MY BREATH AWAY
THE GHOST OF CHRISTMAS PAST
TRUE LOVE WAYS
ANNA'S RETURN
LOVING PROTECTOR
THE FUTURE MRS. WINTER
A PLACE OF PEACE
THE DARK MARSHES

THE BOBBIE BLANDFORD SERIES:
THE LAST DANCE
RUNAWAY

SALLY QUILFORD

---◆---

BIG GIRLS DON'T CRY

Complete and Unabridged

LINFORD
Leicester

First published in Great Britain

First Linford Edition
published 2016

A catalogue record for this book is available
from the British Library.

ISBN 978–1–4448–2948–8

Published by
F. A. Thorpe (Publishing)
Anstey, Leicestershire

Set by Words & Graphics Ltd.
Anstey, Leicestershire
Printed and bound in Great Britain by
T. J. International Ltd., Padstow, Cornwall

This book is printed on acid-free paper

1

'Let me drive, Alf,' I begged when the call about the bank robbery came in. 'Please.'

We had been sent over to the hamlet of Little Stony to investigate a break-in at Mrs Marrick's house, which was next door to the church. It had once been a vicarage, but the vicar had moved into a modern concrete and glass house on the other side of the street. Personally I preferred the old vicarage, with its castellated chimney stacks and arched windows. A keystone over the door said it had been built in 1837. Mrs Marrick lived there with her sister-in-law, Miss Hooper. I guessed them to be in their late sixties. They had a hard life, keeping up maintenance of the house and garden, so both were weather-beaten and tired-looking.

'I had just got out of bed at five

o'clock this morning and I noticed the back door was open,' said Miss Hooper. She was a slender woman with wraith-like arms and a nervous disposition. As she explained what had happened, she fiddled with her fingers, as if holding invisible rosary beads. 'We're supposed to be at the market this morning, but we were afraid to leave the house until you came.'

'Is it possible that you left the door open when you went to bed?' I asked. Back in the '60s, Stony End and its surrounding area was the sort of place where people never locked their doors. Everyone trusted everyone else.

'We never leave the doors unlocked,' said Mrs Marrick. She was larger than her sister-in-law; a buxom woman who put me in mind of an old schoolteacher who had terrorised myself and my friends throughout infant school. I had to remind myself I was a grown-up now and didn't have to be afraid. Mrs Marrick was abrupt, but she had warm grey eyes that softened her forbidding appearance. 'It isn't safe.'

'Really? Have you had any threats?' asked Alf.

'No, nothing like that. I just think we have to do our bit to prevent crime.' Mrs Marrick relented a little, as if she realised she had been unnecessarily cold. 'And some people don't realise that this is no longer a vicarage. They think we keep copious amounts of communion wine.'

'The old reverend was high church,' said Miss Hooper, as if that explained it all. 'Not like the new one. Very progressive, he is.'

My mother, who brought me up alone, had not been particularly religious, apart from at Easter and Christmas, so I did not know the difference between high church and low church. I knew that the new vicar in Little Stony was young and very good-looking, and that had caused suspicion amongst the parishioners, who felt sure he must be the devil in disguise.

'Is anything missing from your

house?' I asked.

'No, nothing that we can see.'

'Anything from outside?'

'No, nothing.'

'We'll take a statement from you both and then send someone up here to get fingerprints,' said Alf. 'If you can make sure you don't touch anything . . . ' As he spoke, we heard a garbled sound coming from outside.

'Is that the radio?' I asked.

'Sounds like it,' said Alf. 'Excuse me, ladies.' In those days, the only police radios we had were in the patrol cars. Personal radios for police officers were not implemented till the late 1960s. As such, we either relied on the car radio, or we had 'points' — usually telephone boxes, either public or those associated with the Tardis from *Doctor Who* — where we had to check in at regular intervals.

Alf came back two minutes later, his face a mixture of horror and excitement. 'There's been a bank robbery in Stony End. We have to leave.'

'Oh how awful,' said Miss Hooper. 'Just like — '

'I'm sure they don't want to know about that, dear,' said Mrs Marrick.

Not really taking in what they had said, I jumped into the Zephyr, raring to go, whilst Alf apologised to the ladies for leaving them. He promised to send someone to follow up their complaint as soon as possible.

The sarge had let us take the black Zephyr because, despite it being early spring, there had been heavy snow on the tops, and it was felt that my Vespa and Alf's pushbike would not quite make the trip to Little Stony. Now the Zephyr was needed for more pressing duties. We had to be discreet in front of the ladies, but as Alf jumped into the car and I set off, switching on the siren, I could not help squealing. 'A bank robbery, Alf! A real life bank robbery. This is what I've been waiting for.'

I spent most of my time doing things like hunting down lost dogs — the last one had ended up living with me and my landlady, Annabel North, for a while; or catching runaway cars — which was how I met the gorgeous doctor, Leo Stanhope, who had become my boyfriend. So a bank robbery seemed like a luxury. Nothing that exciting ever happened in Stony End. True, there had been a few murders, but somehow a bank robbery was more glamorous. When we set out that day, I had visions of a Robin Hood and his Merry Men type of gang, robbing from the rich to feed the poor. The truth would turn out to be far less romantic and much more vicious.

'Just steady on, lass,' Alf said. 'We don't want to end up in a ditch.'

As we drew nearer to Stony End, the snow began to disappear, leaving the beautiful but sometimes bleak landscape of the Peak District ahead of us. In summer it would look different again, but for now the moors stretched out for miles, doing nothing to prevent the cold blast of the wind from seeping through any gaps in the Zephyr. As the only car at the station — meaning it got a lot of use — there were plenty of those. Only my enthusiasm for the chase kept me warm.

'We might be able to stop them leaving town,' I said to Alf, 'if they come this way.'

'Let's hope they don't use any of the other roads leading out of Stony End then,' he said wryly.

'Oh, where's your sense of adventure?' I asked.

'I had enough of that last time there was a bank robbery in Stony End.'

'Really? When?' I turned to look at him.

'Watch out!' Alf cried.

I slammed on the brakes just in time, avoiding hitting the herd of cows that had just come out onto the road, bustled by a local farmer appropriately called Mr Giles.

I opened the window. 'Mr Giles, we're in rather a hurry.'

'You try telling them that,' he said, pointing to the cows.

What followed was an agonising five minutes as the cows moved across the road from one field to another. One stopped right in the middle of the road, looking at us.

'Oh now he's just pulling our leg,' I groaned. 'Come on.' I pipped the horn and switched on the siren.

The cow, completely unimpressed, replied with a lazy, 'Mooooo.'

★   ★   ★

It was early 1962. The winter was fairly mild, and nothing compared to the winter that we would face going into 1963; but in the Peak District, when the wind blew just right — something they call the wind-chill factor nowadays — you could easily think you were in the arctic.

That's how I felt when I finally got out of the Zephyr at Stony End station. Detective Sergeant Miller was waiting for us, smoking a cigarette and shivering. I knew it was not the cold that got to Miller. He would be fine when the pub opened at lunch-time and he could get his first pint of the day.

'You're too late,' he grumbled as I tossed him the keys to the Zephyr. 'What kept you?'

'Cows,' I replied. 'They overpowered us, sir. We didn't stand a chance.'

'Only in Stony End,' he said, rolling his eyes. 'The sarge says you're to come with me, Blandford.'

'Really?' I brightened up. After two years as a probationary officer, I was used to being pushed to the sidelines when there were big cases. Now my probation was over, and being involved in such an exciting case was a big step up for me. I got into the passenger seat of the Zephyr — there's no way Miller would ever have let me drive; his ego couldn't have coped — and we made our way to the bank.

Stony End is a small town in the Peak District, along the Stockport Road. It is in Derbyshire, but we could see both Yorkshire and Lancashire across the peaks. We had exactly one pub, one greasy spoon café, one chip shop, municipal baths called the Slipper Baths, and a Woolworths and Boots. On the high street were several terraced cottages, some of which opened as tearooms for hikers and climbers during the summer months, but it was too early for that. We also had a small cinema, which on that day was showing a double bill of *The Children's Hour* and *Victim*. I had not had a chance to see either, but like many women at the time I had high hopes of marrying Dirk Bogarde, having seen him sacrifice all in *A Tale of Two Cities*. Failing that, I'd have settled for having Audrey Hepburn's gamine figure. At a smidgeon under five feet four (I'd stretched up on my toes a bit at my police medical), with what they euphemistically called child-bearing hips, I doubted I'd ever be like the divine Audrey.

Neither would I be bearing any children at the rate I was going. It reminded me that it was time Leo Stanhope — a dead ringer for a young Richard Burton — and I went out again. We had to be together sometimes to have a relationship, and that just was not happening. With his work as a doctor and mine as a policewoman, our hours did not always coincide. All we managed were snatched moments here and there, and I was afraid it was not enough to sustain a love affair. Our relationship had already taken a couple of batterings: first, when I thought he murdered my father, and then when it appeared that he already had a wife — neither of which was conducive to a successful romance. I could not help wondering what this year would bring to test our resolve.

My landlady, Dr Annabel North, and I had a rule, a while before the Four Seasons sang about it, that big girls did not cry. We might emote elegantly like Katharine Hepburn (we wished!), and sometimes we even beat the stuffing out of our pillows. But we did not cry, no matter what the state of our love life. We were sure that if we said it often enough, it would become true.

I don't say that all this passed

through my mind as we made our way to the bank. It is just a snapshot of where I was in my career and love life on that day. All was about to change, and not for the better.

Miller was not a great talker, and we did not have the rapport that I shared with my friend and mentor, Alf Norris. Alf was like a favourite uncle, and his Austrian wife, Greta, a loving aunt. Miller was more like the drunken uncle that no one really liked but everyone had to invite for Christmas dinner because he gave off such an air of loneliness. So we travelled to the bank in silence. Leo was already there, with an ambulance, tending to the injured. The assistant manager, a middle-aged man called Mr Austin Preston, had been coshed by a bank robber, and was bleeding from his head.

I saw someone I knew standing on the steps, smoking a cigarette. It was Verity, a young girl I had rather clumsily helped in my first year at Stony End, when she had been homeless. She had been at the bank for over a year. Though trying to look mature and self-assured in a tight-fitting blue suit with high-heeled shoes, Verity was only about seventeen years of age. I know she had endured a lot in her short time on earth, and hoped that the bank robbery would not put her off from staying on the straight and narrow.

'What happened?' I asked her.

She was just about to answer, when Miller cut in. 'Leave it to me, Blandford. You just take notes. Can you tell me what happened, Miss — erm . . .'

'Foster,' she replied, blowing smoke rings from her lips in a nonchalant manner that suggested she was very nervous indeed. I did not think Foster was Verity's real surname, but as she had never told us what that was, I wrote it down anyway. She did not trust men like Miller, for reasons she had only hinted to me. So when she did not answer immediately, I gently urged her from behind Miller's back, smiling and nodding my head encouragingly.

'There were four of them. They came

in wearing masks,' she said eventually.

'Stockings?' Miller suggested.

'No, proper masks,' she said. 'Of Frank Sinatra.'

'What?' Miller did not seem to believe her.

Another nod from me, and Verity was happy to reply to Miller's question. 'One of them wore a Frank Sinatra mask. The others had different masks on, though I couldn't see them all properly. We thought it was some sort of prank — I mean, you don't expect bank robberies in Stony End. But then one of them pulled out a gun, and then the others did. They said something like 'Give us all your money' to Mr Preston. He argued, and that's when they hit him. We didn't argue after that; we just handed the money over. We thought they were going to shoot us.'

'How much do you think they got away with?' asked Miller.

Verity looked at me for confirmation that she should speak. 'All the payroll for Mappings for a start. A couple of thousand pounds or more.'

Mappings was a brewery standing high on a hill overlooking Stony End. It had also been the site of my first big case, when the owner, Lionel Mapping, had been found drowned in a vat of beer. Out of the corner of my eye, I noticed Leo pause in his care of Mr Preston. He had good reason: he had been one of the suspects. As I have already said, our relationship had gone through some rocky times.

'Is that a regular thing?' Miller asked Verity.

'Every Friday morning the van from Mappings comes and takes the money up to the factory,' I said.

Miller turned to me, seemingly irritated that I had answered instead of Verity. 'Who knows this?'

'Everyone does, sir.'

'Everyone at the bank?'

'No, everyone in Stony End,' I said, speaking as if to a child. 'Most of the people in the town work for Mappings. But anyone who comes to the market on a Friday can see the Mappings van arrive.'

It was driven by a Mappings employee, and the secretary, a young woman called Miss Bates, went into the bank, flanked by two other brewery employees, and then left with the money in a sack. The same routine every week, without fail. There were no electronic transfers in those days.

Miller swore. 'So it can't have been an inside job, then.'

'I don't know about that,' said Verity. 'They coshed Mr Preston and forced him to give them the code, then they threatened the rest of us. He only gave the information to save us.'

'Where is the manager?'

'Mr Ives is off on account of his wife being in hospital. She crashed her car the other day.'

'I remember that,' I said. 'It happened at the crossroads.' I'd had to direct traffic until the road had been cleared. It brought back memories of my first day on the job, two years before, when I had also had to direct traffic. It occurred to me that my life had not changed that much, despite coming off probation.

'I'd better speak to Preston.' Miller turned towards the ambulance.

Mr Preston groaned. He was sitting in the back of the ambulance, but his face had turned grey. Leo was trying to persuade him to lie down. He mumbled something, to which Leo replied, 'I know, I know. But we'll find them.' After that, Mr Preston became unconscious and was taken to the hospital.

'What did he say, Dr Stanhope?' asked Miller.

'Something about them all being victims,' said Leo.

2

'Right, Blandford, you carry on taking notes, and I'll ask the questions,' said Miller. 'Before we start, let's get things straight. I don't need you to show me how clever you are. I know the sarge rates you, but some of us are good enough on our own.'

'Yes, sir,' I mumbled, almost biting the end of my pencil off in frustration.

Leo, who had tended to some of the other tellers and customers, most of whom were in shock, came over. 'Can you come up tonight?' he asked me. 'Joe's home from school and he wants to speak to us both.'

'That sounds ominous,' I said. 'Is he OK?'

'Yes; never seen him happier, actually. But he won't tell me what it is until you're there.'

Joe Garland was seventeen years old

and Leo's half-brother. They had different mothers but the same father. As Joe's mother had ended up in a psychiatric home, Leo had been caring for him. Only a few months previously, Joe had run away and Leo and I had to go and find him. I'd been running away myself at the time, so I knew how Joe felt. But things had been good since we both returned, as far as I could tell. I hoped that we were not heading into another bout of teenage angst.

'When you've finished sorting out your love life, Blandford . . . ' said Miller.

'Yes, sir.'

There were three tellers in the bank. Verity was one of them; then there was Mrs Olive Green and Mrs June Ogden. Mrs Green and Mrs Ogden were of a similar type. Both wore twinset and pearls, with a tweed skirt, and both had tightly permed hair, though Mrs Green's hair was blue-rinsed and Mrs Ogden's was dark brown. I suspected they went shopping together regularly. They even wore the same shoes — brown lace-up brogues.

They could have been sisters, but they were not.

'It was awful,' said Mrs Green.

'Dreadful,' said Mrs Ogden.

'I thought I was going to die,' Mrs Green said.

'I'm sure he was aiming at me,' said Mrs Ogden. 'Not you, dear.'

'Well, no dear, the gun was pointed in my direction.'

'Can you give us an idea what sort of a gun it was?' asked Miller.

'I'm sure I don't know the makes of guns,' said Mrs Green with a disgusted sniff.

'If my Jimmy were here, he could tell you,' said Mrs Ogden. 'He's an expert in these things.' Mrs Ogden could often be heard telling tales of her son and how clever he was at everything. From what I knew of him, Jimmy Ogden had spent most of his life on the dole, and still lived with his mother.

'But Jimmy wasn't in the bank?' asked Miller.

'Well no, of course not.'

'So what use is he?' muttered Miller.

'Was there anything familiar about the robbers?' I asked, earning a warning glance from Miller. I felt he was letting the women twitter away without learning anything.

'Only insomuch as they were wearing masks of Frank Sinatra, Dean Martin, Peter Lawford and . . . who is that black one?' Mrs Green's brow furrowed. 'Nice dancer. He's been on Sunday Night at the London Palladium once or twice.'

'Sammy Davis Jr,' said Mrs Ogden.

'It's just like *Ocean's Eleven*,' I said.

'Oh, no, dear,' said Mrs Green. 'There were only four of them.'

'Yes, but those actors were in the film *Ocean's Eleven*.'

'But he was black,' said Mrs Ogden.

'Yes, Sammy Davis Jr is black,' I agreed.

'No, I mean the person under the mask was. I saw his neck.'

'Did you?' Mrs Green looked at her friend quizzically. 'I can't say I noticed. I saw there were two older men and two younger men.'

'Oh yes, dear. I'm sure he was black.

It'll be that Clyde Smith who works at Mr Patel's next to the prefabs.'

'Really? I'll go and speak to him,' said Miller.

'But sir,' I protested, 'just because one of the robbers might have been black doesn't mean it was Clyde Smith.'

'He's the only one living nearby.'

'That still doesn't mean it's him.' I wanted to ask more about the men and how Mrs Green could tell their ages. I believed it was more likely to help us find the men, but Miller had the bit between his teeth and I feared he would not let go.

'He's been in trouble before, Blandford, before you came to Stony End. Come on, we'll go and find him. We'll have this wrapped up by teatime.' Miller told Mrs Green and Mrs Ogden to call in at the station and give their statements, then I reluctantly followed him out.

In the 1960s Stony End had a very small ethnic community. They were a quiet hard-working group who did not mix much with the locals. A newly arrived Chinese couple had bought the chip shop from my mother's friend, Dottie Riley. They had only been there a month or two, so we didn't know much about them. Mr Patel, on the other hand, was a well-known figure in Stony End. He ran a corner shop out of one of the old prefabs, not far from where Alf and Greta Norris lived.

When we arrived at the shop, Clyde Smith was emptying the van and carrying goods inside. I can still see the shop in my mind's eye. Sweet jars on the shelves behind the counter. Fresh vegetables were laid out on trays. None of your perfectly straight carrots or cleaned potatoes. The produce still smelled of the fields from where it came. The shelves were laden with Heinz Beans, Spam, Campbell's soups, dried peas, and fresh uncut Hovis bread. Sliced bread was still treated suspiciously by many, and generally considered to be the lazy way of doing things, but there were a few sliced loaves of Mother's Pride for those in a hurry.

'Clyde Smith?' asked Miller.

Clyde looked at Miller warily. He was a very tall and handsome boy of about eighteen, with coffee-coloured skin and startling blue eyes.

'Yes, Mr Miller.'

'Where have you been all day?'

'He's been to the cash and carry for me,' said Mr Patel, coming in from the back room. A portly man in his fifties, he had kind brown eyes. He often let the poorer families have food on the tab and was not too worried if they didn't pay him back in double-quick time. He knew that eventually they would have to use his shop again, so would pay him to save the embarrassment of owing the money. There were not many other options in Stony End. Something of an entrepreneur, Mr Patel owned the shop and lots of rental properties around town, having moved there from Pakistan before the war.

'You've been seen,' said Miller. I wanted to protest, but his eyes warned me otherwise.

'Where? I haven't been in trouble since I was sixteen,' said Clyde. 'I swear, Mr Miller.'

'He's a good, hard-working boy,' said Mr Patel. 'Leave him alone.'

'Do you want to be done for aiding and abetting?' asked Miller.

'Sir,' I managed to croak.

'Not a word, Blandford, or you'll be on probation again.'

'But sir . . . ' I wished Alf were with me. He knew how to ask questions in a way that didn't make everyone feel immediately guilty of some crime they had not committed.

'So I'll ask again,' said Miller, ignoring me. 'Where were you today?'

'I've been to the cash and carry in the big town,' said Clyde.

'Did anyone see you?'

'Of course they did. I sort of stand out in a crowd, in case you hadn't noticed.'

'Don't get smart with me, boy.'

I cringed then, and I still cringe now, when I think of how Miller behaved towards Clyde. I'm glad to say that Miller was rare amongst those who lived in Stony End. I had once been told that Stony End was the place you came when you had nowhere else to go, and as such, people, no matter what colour their skin, were treated with kindness and respect. True, there was a subsection of people with xenophobic leanings, especially since the war. Nowhere is perfect. But for the most part, everyone in Stony End lived in harmony.

'There's been a robbery at the bank,' said Miller. 'You were recognised.'

'Clyde, don't say another word,' said Mr Patel. 'I will call my solicitor. Just don't speak.'

'I haven't done anything,' said Clyde.

'Hush now,' Mr Patel cautioned.

Everything happened very quickly after that. Clyde suddenly took flight, dashing past me and Miller and jumping into Mr Patel's van before taking off down the road. We set off in pursuit, chasing him over the tops, but he had a good head start on us on account of our being dumbstruck for a few seconds after he tore off down the road. We followed him through the lanes, but he was faster than us, particularly when another herd of cows — or it might have been the same herd; it's hard to tell the difference between cows — cut us off from the chase. Half an hour later, we found the van abandoned on the edge of the peaks on the Stockport road, with no sign of Clyde.

'He's guilty as hell,' said Miller.

'He's frightened as hell,' I said.

'Frightened?'

'Yes, sir, frightened. It was clear you didn't believe him.'

'Why should I? I bet Patel is in on it as well.'

'Sir, you can't just assume it was Clyde Smith because a woman said she saw a bit of black skin. She might have been wrong. Mrs Green didn't notice it.'

'That lot are nothing but trouble, Blandford. And the sooner you realise it, the better.'

'That lot?'

'The blacks and the Asians. They ought to go back where they came from.'

'It sounded to me as if Mr Patel and Clyde Smith are from around here. They've both got Derbyshire accents.'

'You know what I mean.'

I did know what he meant, but I did not like it one bit.

'We'll put out a bulletin on Clyde Smith and have that boy locked up by tonight,' said Miller. 'He won't have got far. This case will be solved before you know it, Blandford. Watch and learn. Watch and learn.'

'I've already learned so much from you, sir,' I said, not bothering to hide my ironic tone.

3

'He just automatically assumed it was Clyde,' I said as Leo passed me a dish of mashed potato. He had cooked a roast chicken with stuffing and all the trimmings. When I went to get a bottle of wine, I had seen a fresh trifle in the fridge. I didn't know if Leo was treating me or his brother Joe, but we were both very grateful. 'The poor kid was terrified.'

'It could be Clyde,' said Joe.

'Joe!' I said, disappointed. 'I didn't think you were like that.'

'No, not because of his colour,' said Joe, blushing. 'We've got boys from all over the world at my school. Sons of diplomats and all that. I mean . . . ' He looked glum. 'He's been seeing Verity.'

'Oh.'

'So he might have been trying to get information from her, that's what I'm saying.' He sounded unconvinced.

'Or maybe,' Leo said gently, 'because you like her, you hope it's something like that.'

'Yeah, maybe,' said Joe, nodding. 'Sorry. Clyde's all right, really. He's not the one who was knocking her about last year. When I had that trouble with those other boys on the estate, he was OK with me. I used to go and get stuff for Mr Rodgers from the shop.'

Mr Rodgers was a disabled serviceman whom Joe had helped out as a sort of penance the year before, after vandalising Mr Rodgers's property. They had become good friends. Mr Rodgers had decided to move away from Stony End and go to live on the coast to get away from some bad memories. I think Joe still missed him.

'So how is school?' I asked, silently kicking myself. Asking about school was what you did with a child or teenager when you didn't know how else to connect to them.

'Good, yeah. Really good.'

'Joe's been getting some great results in his tests, and there's a chance of a scholarship to Oxford,' said Leo proudly.

'That's wonderful!' I said. 'Well done, Joe.' Given the problems Joe had endured in his young life, this was a real achievement. Things could have been very different. Leo had been a real tearaway as a teenager, and it was only as he matured that he settled down to become a doctor.

'That's what I wanted to talk to you both about,' said Joe.

'Go on then,' said Leo warily.

'Let's finish dinner first,' said Joe. It was clear he was trying to put off what he wanted to say. We knew better than to push him to speak, so we did as he asked. Dinner was a lively affair as we discussed the new films and a plan to go to the pictures together whilst Joe was off school. Joe and Leo wanted to go and see John Wayne in *The Comancheros*, whereas I wanted to see Rock Hudson and Doris Day in *Lover Come Back to Me*. Never the twain shall meet, as they say. We did all manage to agree that *The*

Day the Earth Caught Fire, starring Leo McKern, might be worth watching if it came to town.

'Anything would be better than those boring films on at the moment,' said Joe. He made a yawning motion, patting his mouth with his hand.

'Don't you disrespect Dirk Bogarde in my hearing,' I quipped. I could understand that both *Victim* and *The Children's Hour* might seem a bit dull and worthy for a seventeen-year-old boy.

Afterwards, Leo and I went into the drawing room with our coffee, whilst Joe had a bottle of Pepsi Cola. He put some music on the record player. 'Runaway' by Del Shannon struck up, reminding me of my flight to Scarborough the year before. It had not been a happy time for me. 'Have you got anything else?' I asked. So Joe put on Gene Pitney's 'A Town Without Pity'. I'm sure that, at least at that moment, we were happier than the music suggests, but I still feel a pang in my throat when I remember those two songs. The latter song in particular was going to have some meaning as the year wore on and some uncomfortable truths came out.

Stanhope Manor was a fine old house, set high on a hill overlooking the town. I'd be lying if I said that I hadn't dreamed of living there someday. Not just because of the house, but because I loved Leo and wanted to marry him. The drawing room was some twenty-five feet long and fifteen feet wide, with heavy oak furniture dating back to Georgian times. There was a red velvet sofa either side of the roaring fire. We all sat there, drinking coffee, and full to the brim with crispy roast chicken and sherry trifle. Except for Joe, who couldn't sit still for more than a couple of minutes. I put it down to youthful energy.

'Do you want a beer, Leo?' asked Joe. 'What about a Babycham, Bobbie? Or a Snowball? Anything? I'll get it.' He was definitely on edge.

'I'm beginning to wonder what you're putting off,' Leo said, laughing. 'Just tell us. Is it a girl, Joe? Because whatever has happened, we'll help you to work it out.'

'No, it's not a girl.' Joe tsked and rolled his eyes. 'I never get the girl. I thought you knew that.'

'Oh dear,' I said, trying not to laugh. I remembered what it was to be seventeen, where relationships were the be-all and end-all of one's life. Who am I kidding? I felt the same way, and I defy any woman who's ever felt differently to say otherwise. It did matter then, and it matters to young girls now, even though it shouldn't. 'There will be someone for you, Joe. You're handsome and clever, just like your big brother.'

'There's no need to humour me, Bobbie,' said Joe, but he was grinning and looked pleased with what I had said. 'It's about school,' he said at last.

'You're doing well, aren't you?' asked Leo. 'Your housemaster tells me you're in the top four of your class.'

'I'm the top, actually.'

'Well then. No trouble from the other boys?'

'No, Leo. I'm fine. No one's picking on me. I'm doing well in my classes. Like you said, I've got the chance of a scholarship to Oxford.'

'So what's the problem?' I asked.

Joe took a deep breath. 'I don't want to go to Oxford.'

'Fair enough,' said Leo. 'You could try for Cambridge. Or if you don't want an Oxbridge university . . . '

'I don't want to go to university, Leo.'

'Right . . . ' Leo sounded doubtful.

'That's why I wanted Bobbie to be here too. Because she can advise me what I need to do.'

'I don't know how I can, Joe,' I said. 'I don't know anything about university life or what other options are open to you.'

'Yes you do,' said Joe. 'You know everything there is to know about joining the police force.'

'What?' said Leo, frowning.

He might have been perplexed, but it was starting to become clear to me. 'You want to join the police force?' I said. I clapped my hands together. 'That's wonderful, Joe! You're just the sort of bright young man the force needs. In fact there are more opportunities for you than for me. I'd be jealous, but I'm too thrilled you're taking this route.'

'It's because of you, Bobbie,' said Joe. 'You've inspired me to want to help people and fight for justice. I want to join up and help people like you do.'

I smiled, remembering my own ideals when I first started out. Some of them had taken a severe beating, but I didn't say that to Joe. He would have to learn himself. Or maybe he wouldn't. Maybe he could do more than I ever could. As we chatted away about Joe's possibilities, I became aware that Leo had not spoken at all. Joe finally noticed too.

'So, Leo,' he said, 'what do you think?'

Leo expelled a burst of air from his

mouth, as if he had been holding his breath till that moment. 'I don't know what to think, Joe,' he said. 'Only . . . No, I have to say this.' He shook his head vehemently. 'As your legal guardian, I disagree. You can't just give up on your education like that. Why on earth would you want to throw away your chances and join the police force?'

I don't know how Joe felt about what Leo said, but I felt as though I'd been slapped in the face to the extent that the coffee cup I held fell into my lap, spilling the dregs all over my skirt. 'Oh silly me,' I said, trying to hide my hurt and confusion behind embarrassed laughter.

'I'll get you a cloth,' said Joe. He practically ran from the room as if to escape the heavy atmosphere.

'Bobbie? Are you OK?' asked Leo. 'Have you scalded yourself?' He went to take my hand, but I snatched it away.

'No, no, I'm fine. The coffee was cold. I'm just clumsy and stupid, that's all.'

'Of course you're not stupid.'

Joe came back with a cloth and I wiped my skirt. What I really wanted to do was run out of there and go home to lick my wounds, but pride prevented me.

'It's what I want to do, Leo,' Joe said to his brother.

'After what your mother sacrificed . . . '

'Don't give me that. Don't ever use my mother to shame me. I thought you were better than that!' Joe stormed from the room. I heard his footsteps clumping up the stairs and then on the ceiling above us.

'That went well,' said Leo in a wry tone. I didn't reply. 'You can see what I mean though, can't you, Bobbie?'

'It's nothing to do with me,' I said, barely able to move my mouth, my lips felt so tight.

'Well it is, in a way. Can't you have a word with him, and tell him he needs to consider other options?'

'More suited to his class, you mean?'

'That isn't what I meant, Bobbie.'

'Well what did you mean, Leo?

You've just dismissed my career as being worthless, so clearly you think it's beneath anyone in your family to do it.' I stood up. 'I'm tired. I'm going home.'

Leo stood up too. 'You know damn well that I didn't mean that.'

'Do I, Leo? Because it sounded to me as if it's exactly what you meant. It's a wonder you can bring yourself to speak to me.'

'Now you're being ridiculous.'

'Well that's what comes of having no education and a worthless career.'

'For God's sake!' Leo threw up his arms. 'I can't talk to you when you're like this.'

'Well, don't talk to me, then.' I made for the front door. My Vespa was parked outside. I jumped onto it and took off into the night, hoping that the icy air would cool my flaming temper.

★   ★   ★

'He said what?' said Annabel when I'd blurted out the whole story to her over a late-night cup of Horlicks. Leo had telephoned to make sure I got home safely, but it was fair to say that our conversation had been pitched somewhere between Greenland and the North Pole.

I sat on the sofa, cuddling Elvis. No, not that one. Dottie Riley's dog, Elvis. He had lived with us for several months the previous year when Dottie had gone into hiding over a former indiscretion. Even though Dottie had come home, Elvis had judiciously decided to give us joint custody, moving deftly between Annabel's cottage and Dottie's new place at the pub; mainly because it got him extra dinners and treats. For a big black dog of no discernible heritage, he was pretty smart.

'He said that Joe could do so much better than the police force. So where does that leave me, Annabel? Does he mean that the police force is a worthless occupation, full stop? Or does he think it's just good enough for me because I'm a woman?'

'Oh darling, that's awful,' she said. As two women in a man's world, Annabel and I often stood shoulder to shoulder against chauvinism. I had to put up with it in the police force and Annabel had to put up with it as a female doctor in a male-dominated realm.

But I had never expected Leo to look down on me. In the past he had been supportive of my career. The idea that he saw it as a lesser calling had never occurred to me. 'I know he wants the best for Joe,' I said to Annabel. 'But the way he talked about being in the police . . . it shocked me that he felt that way. I had no idea he could be such a snob!'

'What are you going to do?'

'There's nothing I can do. I'm sick of trying to prove myself, and I never thought I'd have to do it with Leo.'

'Are you going to finish with him?'

'Again?' I sighed, remembering all our other break-ups. 'Sometimes I wonder if we even got started. There have been so many problems. I wonder if it's worth all the hassle just to keep hitting another brick wall on the merry-go-round.' It's fair to say that I was prone to mixing my metaphors.

'Do you love him?'

'Yes. But I'm not sure love is always enough when there are so many other differences.'

We didn't break up officially, but our busy lives made it difficult for us to overcome our difference of opinion regarding Joe. We saw each other, but we were never together long enough to talk things through. If he was not called to the hospital, I was called out on a case. We merely drifted along, with his words like an open wound that would not heal. He still did not understand how what he said might have hurt me, and in the spirit of female thinking throughout the ages, I was determined that if he didn't know, I wasn't going to tell him.

One day, not long afterwards, Joe came to see me at the station and took away some leaflets about joining the force. 'I was going to chuck school,' he admitted. 'But then I realised that would be really stupid, especially with my exams so near. So I'm leaving things for a while to give Leo time to get used to the idea.'

'You are a bright boy,' I said.

'You know he didn't mean it the way it sounded, don't you, Bobbie?' asked Joe.

'I'm not sure he could have meant it any other way.'

'He's really proud of you and all you've achieved.'

'You mean what with me being a mere woman and all that?' I coughed, choking on my own self-pity. 'Sorry, Joe, I didn't mean to get all bitter with you. Good luck with your exams.'

Joe's visit was closely followed by one from Mrs Higgins. Martha Higgins was one of my favourite people in Stony End, and one of the first I made friends with when I arrived. As mad as a hatter, with outlandish clothing to match, Mrs Higgins had a very strange relationship with the truth. Yet she was one of the most honest people I knew. She often saw the truth where a lot of others didn't.

'I hear there's trouble at t'mill,' she said, affecting a more northern accent than usual. She handed over a banana cake wrapped in brown paper. 'I made this for you.'

'Thank you. Trouble at what mill?' I asked.

'Between you and the handsome doctor.'

'We're fine,' I lied.

'That's not what Dr North said when she came to check on my bad knee.'

'What exactly has Annabel said?' I asked, determined not to be caught out. Mrs Higgins had a way of pretending she knew things in advance so that you slipped up and told her what she had wanted to know all along.

'Well she didn't say anything. But that's sometimes all you need. When I worked for the resistance during the war, interrogating Nazi swine, it was the things people didn't say that mattered most. That's how I knew to tell Barnes

Wallace and his people to bomb the dams. I even went up in a plane with Guy Gibson. Not on the actual run. Just the practice.'

I shook my head to try and get rid of the image of Mrs Higgins flying a Lancaster over the Lady Bower reservoir.

'Anyway, I've seen you both together lately,' she continued. 'Faces as long as wet weekends, you've had.'

'I'm fine, Mrs Higgins, really. Leo's fine. Everything's fine.'

'Fine,' she echoed, slapping the desk. 'Oh, you'll want this.' She handed over another brown paper package. It was flatter than the cake, though slightly lumpy. 'I haven't touched it. I found it on my compost heap and picked it up with rubber gloves.'

'What is it?'

I opened the package to find a Frank Sinatra mask.

4

Consumed by my own problems, I had almost forgotten the bank robbery. The rest of the country had not, and of course, several police forces were still investigating. The newspapers ran stories about the robbers as if they were heroes, and despite Mr Preston being hurt, lots of people were of the mind that if they could commit a bank robbery and get away with it, they would.

We did a search of Mrs Higgins's compost heap and surrounding areas, but didn't find anything else of note. The mask was sent away for testing, but it was fair to say that after several days of rain and sleet and whatever nasty things she'd thrown on the heap, any forensic evidence was long since compromised.

Clyde Smith was still missing, so he

was considered public enemy number one by everyone but me and Verity Foster. His picture had been distributed throughout the country. When another bank robbery, by the same gang, took place near Sheffield, Scotland Yard became involved. We were warned that they would be sending one of their finest to take over the case.

'So we want all those files and statements in good order,' said Sergeant Jack Simmonds during a briefing on the case. We were in his office at the time, several of us crammed into the relatively small room. All the rooms at Stony End police station were small, so nowhere else would have been any better.

The sarge was a fine-looking man in his fifties. He could be irascible and didn't suffer fools gladly, but he was also a good commander to his men (and woman). We could tell by his voice that he was not happy to have the case swept from under him. We may have done things slowly in Stony End, but we usually got results. We had come to believe that our slow work lulled criminals into a false sense of security, which in turn led to them making silly mistakes. 'Go back to all the witnesses and ask them again what they saw. And find Clyde Smith!'

'Sarge,' I said, 'I don't think he's guilty. He's just scared.'

'Well then he needs to come forward so we can prove he didn't do it,' said the sarge. 'I know how you feel about this, Blandford, because of his colour, and I agree we can't convict him on that point alone. But he didn't do himself any favours by running.'

I had to admit the sarge had a point. 'He was seeing Verity Foster,' I said. 'I'll go and ask if she knows where he is.'

'It's not natural,' said Miller. 'A white girl with a boy . . . like that.'

'Her love life is not our business,' said the sarge. 'But we do need to speak to him. Go on, Blandford. She trusts you.'

'She won't if we lock her boyfriend up,' I muttered.

Verity lodged in a boarding house on the edge of Stony End. It was the sort of prim and proper place that doesn't exist anymore, where young ladies lived in almost nun-like seclusion, apart from when they went out to work. They had to be in by a certain time at night, and were not allowed to invite men into the house. Nor were they allowed to get drunk or bring alcohol onto the premises. Any breach of the rules could lead to them being evicted, after which it might be difficult to find another place to take them. Not for the first time, I gave thanks for being able to live with Annabel in her comfortable cottage, where we kept our own hours, and a medicinal Babycham was always on offer.

I was shown up to Verity's bedroom. She had made some attempts to turn it into a home by adding little ornaments and soft furnishings. A pale blue scarf with tassels hung over the lampshade. Posters of Elvis Presley and James Dean adorned the walls, along with film posters of Steve McQueen in *The Blob* and Gregory Peck and Audrey Hepburn in *Roman Holiday*.

'You've got it looking really homely,' I said. There was only one chair, so I had that, whilst Verity sat on the bed. 'It's about Clyde,' I said. 'We need to speak to him, Verity.'

'He had nothing to do with it, and neither did I,' she said. She lounged on her bed, wearing black pedal-pushers and a black sleeveless sweater. With her long, slender legs and flat tummy, Verity could have given Audrey Hepburn a run for her money in the looks department.

We had already established Verity's innocence in a previous meeting. She did not know the combination of the safe at the bank, and it was unlikely, given her position as a junior clerk, that either Mr Preston or Mr Ives would have given it to her. Though Verity had lived on the streets for a while, and had made some mistakes in her life, she was not the femme fatale type.

'He isn't helping his case by hiding, Verity,' I said, echoing the sarge's words. 'Why did he run away?'

'Because that Miller was out to get him, that's why.'

'So you've spoken to Clyde?' I said gently, slightly ashamed about catching her out.

'He telephoned me. Look . . . ' She lowered her voice. 'If the matron finds out I'm seeing him, she'll throw me out.'

'Why? You're not forbidden from having boyfriends. Only from bringing them back to your room.'

'But Clyde is different,' she muttered. 'The matron thinks we should stick to our own kind. I can't risk her throwing me out. I can't afford to stay anywhere else, and I'd lose my job.'

'I know it's hard. But Verity, if you speak to Clyde again, tell him to come and speak to the sarge. No one is going to harm him, I promise.'

'You can't promise that,' she said. 'None of you can. Not with people like Miller around.'

51

'We can trust the sarge. He's a good man and only wants to find out the truth. What else can you tell me about that day when the bank was robbed?'

'I've told you everything.'

'Was anyone acting strangely beforehand? Any of the other staff at the bank? Any of the customers?'

'Not really. Mr Preston was stressed because Mr Ives, the manager, was away, but that's all. He's always the same when Mr Ives has time off. He's a fussy little thing.'

'Mr Ives?'

'No, Mr Preston. Always has to have his clothes just so, and doesn't like it if anyone moves things on his desk. He once caught Mrs Ogden with his diary and he threatened to sack her.'

'How is he, do you know?' I knew, but I wanted to test Verity to see if she cared enough to find out.

'He's OK,' Verity replied. 'I went to see him yesterday and took him some grapes. Poor man. I do want them to catch the people who did it, honestly.

Because he's harmless, really.'

There was little more I could get out of Verity, so I said my goodbyes and returned to the station.

Alf Norris was on the desk. 'Psst,' he whispered to me as I walked in. 'They're here.'

'Who's here?'

'Scotland Yard. They're in with the sarge.'

'Already?'

'Yep. I didn't see them, but Ernie Price did just before he went home.' Ernie Price was the night shift desk sergeant. 'I forgot to ask,' Alf continued, 'Greta wants you to come to tea on Sunday. She's heard that Mrs Higgins has made you a cake, so she's been baking for days.'

Mrs Higgins and Greta Norris's competition to win my undying adoration through their cakes had become something of a joke in Stony End. I didn't mind. It meant I got lots of cakes baked for me, and the rest of my friends often benefitted when I shared what I couldn't manage to eat.

'You can bring Leo if you want,' said Alf.

'I'll see,' I said. 'He may be busy.'

'I'd heard there were problems. If you need to talk, lass, you know where I am.'

Sometimes life in Stony End could feel claustrophobic, and this was one of those times. It was nigh-on impossible to have a private life. Alf and Greta might be like a favourite uncle and aunt, but like most young people with the older generation, I could not imagine them being able to understand my romantic problems.

'Thanks Alf, but I'm OK.'

The sarge's door opened and two men wearing long grey overcoats came out. One was in his late twenties, already balding, and wearing horn-rimmed glasses. The other in his early thirties and startlingly handsome, with fair hair and vivid blue eyes. He was the one who got my attention, but not for the reasons you might think.

'Tom!' I exclaimed, practically flying into his arms. 'What are you doing here?'

'I've come to solve your crime for you,' he said, grinning. He held me away from him, looking me up and down in my uniform and nodding his approval. 'Hello, baby sister.'

5

My brother, Tom Blandford, was ten years older than me, and I had always looked up to him. He had attended Hendon Police College and then immediately went into a position of command, ending up at Scotland Yard as a detective chief inspector. Tom had been at the forefront of some of the most famous cases of the '50s and early '60s, including the chase for a double agent. Sadly, the agent had defected to Moscow before Tom could arrest him. It was one of his few failures. As a devoted sister, I had been following his career. I did it with the bittersweet knowledge that as a woman in the police force, I would never be in a position to match his success. Now here he was, in Stony End, taking over the investigation of the bank robbery with his friend.

'This is Detective Carl Latimer,' Tom said, making the introductions. 'Carl, this is my little sister, Bobbie — the scourge of Stony End.' I bristled a bit at the wry introduction, but didn't really think much of it at the time. I was used to my brother teasing me.

Carl Latimer had a good, strong handshake and kind brown eyes. 'Nice to meet you, Bobbie,' he said. 'Tom has told me a lot about you.'

'All good, I hope.'

'Yes, of course. Nothing bad at all. He always speaks very highly of you. You . . . you're lovely. Just like he said.'

'I'll send you a cheque in the post,' I said to Tom.

'Can we get back to the case?' said the sarge. 'Blandford.'

'Yes?' Tom and I said together.

'WPC Blandford,' the sarge said for clarity. 'You've been to see Verity Foster?'

'Yes, Sarge, but she's not saying anything.'

'Is this the girlfriend of the black

boy?' asked Tom. 'The one who's on the run?'

'Yes, that's right,' I replied.

'We need to shake her up a bit,' he said.

'What do you mean, shake her up, Tom?' I asked. 'That's not how we work here.'

'No, that's obvious, sis — otherwise the boy would be in custody. How did you manage to let him get away, Bobbie?'

'I . . . I didn't let him get away.' I was about to say that Miller was doing the driving at the time, but despite my feelings about Miller it felt disloyal to say so. I wanted to protect Stony End station from criticism.

'It doesn't matter now,' said Tom. 'We'll go and see her and get her talking.'

'How exactly do you expect her to do that?' I asked. 'Don't forget, she's only seventeen. If you do question her, I'll have to be there.'

'No, it's all right. You can leave it to

us now,' Tom said. 'We'll make sure there's a responsible adult there.' Something about the way he said it made me doubt that they would.

'I need you to go up to Little Stony and speak to Mrs Marrick and Miss Hooper,' the sarge said to me. 'We still haven't established all the details of their break-in. They've been forgotten, and that's not how we do things here either.'

'So are we not involved in the bank robbery investigation at all?' I asked, glaring at my brother.

'You've done a good job, Bobbie,' Tom said, patting me on the shoulder somewhat patronisingly. 'Not bad at all for an amateur, even if the main suspect did get away.' He winked. 'Now leave it to the professionals. We've dealt with this gang before. We know their methods.'

'You can't frighten Verity,' I warned. 'She's had a tough time in her life.'

'In what way?' asked Latimer.

'Well . . . she used to live on the

streets, but now she's turned her life around.'

'Has a record, does she?' asked Tom.

'Not that I know of,' I said, feeling my face getting hotter and hotter. I began to wish I had not said anything. Miller was bad enough, but my brother's tough style of modern policing would terrify Verity — maybe even cause her to run away again.

'Go up to Little Stony, Blandford,' said the sarge, his brow furrowed. 'Let me deal with our friends from Scotland Yard.'

'Sarge . . .'

He cast me a warning glance, and as he was my superior, there was nothing I could do but obey him.

The snow on the tops had thawed over the past few days, so I took my Vespa up to Little Stony. It was a hamlet not far from Stony End which had a castle that was said to have been important at some time. The previous year we had found a dead body in the grounds. The year before that, an elderly man had been murdered in one of the cottages. For a tiny hamlet, Little Stony saw more than its fair share of drama.

Mrs Marrick and her sister-in-law, Miss Hooper, shared a large detached house at the end of the hamlet. It had its own orchard, and in the summer they grew vegetables in an adjacent smallholding. They sold them on the market, along with jams and chutneys made from the fruits off their trees. Blossom had already begun to grow on the apple and cherry trees. In a few weeks they would be a blaze of colour. Miss Hooper was digging in the smallholding when I arrived. She stopped what she was doing when she saw my Vespa, and waved at me. Mrs Marrick was in the kitchen, baking.

'We have a visitor, dear,' said Miss Hooper as she led me into the kitchen. 'Would you like a cup of tea, WPC Blandford?'

'Thank you, no,' I said. 'I just came to apologise for leaving you both in the lurch the other day. The sarge has asked me to come and finish questioning you about the break-in.'

'Oh that,' said Mrs Marrick, turning from her baking. Her face was flushed from the heat. 'It was a silly mistake, wasn't it, dear?'

'Yes,' said Miss Hooper. 'My fault entirely. I went out early in the morning and left the back door open, and then forgot I'd done it. So I came home and completely frightened myself. I . . . we did mean to tell you, but with everything that's happened in Stony End at the bank, we felt you had enough to do.'

I looked towards the back door, puzzled. 'Didn't you say that the lock had been broken?' Alf and I barely had time to check before the call about the bank robbery came in. I wondered what my brother would say about such shoddy policing, then put him out of my mind. We did have our own way of doing things in Stony End, and even if it was all rather informal, we got results.

'Did I? Oh, I think I might have been

mistaken about that, too.' Miss Hooper giggled like a schoolgirl, but there was something false about it. 'It's funny how the mind plays tricks on one.'

'You said that you thought the drawers had been searched,' I said.

'Probably by me,' said Mrs Marrick. 'I had lost my bank book and spent ages looking for it the night before. I think with the door being open and the drawers still sticking out, it gave Beattie the idea that we'd been burgled. I've had to promise not to frighten her like that again.'

I almost gave them a lecture about wasting police time, but decided against it. I had the feeling something odd was happening, but if they were determined not to make a complaint, there was little I could do. But I did want to find out more about them. I had often seen them at the market. They had a stall like Mrs Higgins's, selling much the same produce. But whereas Mrs Higgins's stall was outside, cluttered and overladen, Mrs Marrick and Miss Hooper's stall was in the built-in market, and very neat and pretty. It tended to attract the better-off residents of Stony End.

'Well, if I don't have to take a statement, perhaps I could have that cuppa,' I suggested cheerfully.

'Of course,' said Mrs Marrick. 'I'll put the kettle on. Beattie, why don't you show WPC Blandford the garden whilst I make the tea?'

I was bustled out of the kitchen and into the garden. Even though the snow had gone, there was still a chill wind blasting across the peaks. Miss Hooper's ruddy face showed a woman who spent most of her life outdoors. I also spent a lot of time outdoors walking on the beat, but it wasn't quite the same as the effort that must go into keeping a smallholding.

'How long have you lived here?' I asked.

'Since early in the war. I came here to get away from the bombing in Sheffield.'

'You and Mrs Marrick are sisters-in-law?'

'Not exactly. We would have been, and so we consider that we are. I was to marry Henri's brother, Harry.'

'Sorry, but who is Henri?'

'Henri . . . Henrietta Marrick.'

'Ah. Sorry, go on. What happened to Harry?' I affected a sympathetic tone. It was never certain, with the war not so far in the past, if people had lost loved ones.

'Nothing happened to him. He's living happily in Skegness with his wife and children. He runs a caravan park there. Anyway, after Harry and I broke up, Henri invited me to stay here. Her husband was away in the war — he died in Africa. I had no one else, and Sheffield was getting bombed to kingdom come. I've been here ever since.'

'What do you do? I've seen you at the market, but I can't imagine that pays much.'

'I have a small annuity left to me by an aunt, and Henri has her own income left to her by her husband, and her widow's pension, of course. We get by.'

'But you're not rich?'

'No, not at all. People assume we are because we live in this big house, but the cost of the upkeep is tremendous. I was a schoolteacher for a while, and during the war Henri worked in a bank.'

'If someone did break in, would there be anything of value for them to take?' I asked. 'Any silver or large amounts of cash?'

'No one broke in, WPC Blandford. It was my silly mistake. I feel quite foolish about it. Ah, I think Henri is calling us in for tea.'

I followed her back to the kitchen, wondering what had really happened. Miss Hooper was certainly the nervous type. But I didn't have her pegged as the type to see something that was not there.

Later, back at the station, the sarge told me to forget it. 'It's probably some family thing. If they don't want to press charges, there's little we can do. We have more important things to worry about.'

'What is it, Sarge?'

'Your brother has arrested Verity Foster for withholding information.'

6

'She's in a cell,' said the sarge. 'I've insisted that he wait until you get back before questioning her, but she's pretty shook up about it. Go in and see if you can calm her down.'

'Yes, Sarge.' I made a cup of tea and cut a slice of the Victoria sponge Mrs Marrick and Miss Hooper had insisted I take away with me. I left the rest in the kitchenette for my colleagues to share and took the slice and the tea to Verity's cell.

As I passed the interrogation room, I heard my brother and Carl Latimer discussing tactics. I hoped they would not see me, but Carl looked up and smiled as I passed. He said nothing to my brother, for which I was grateful.

'We've got to be tough with them,' Tom was saying. 'They're too soft up here. It's time they learned some proper policing.' He did not sound at all like the brother I remembered.

I found Verity in a dreadful state, sobbing her heart out, in the cell. 'I've done nothing wrong!' she cried.

'It's all right, Verity. Have some tea and cake. I'm going to be here to help you.'

She sniffed loudly and wiped her nose on her sleeve. I handed her a clean handkerchief. 'He's a pig,' she said. 'Both of them are.'

'Who?'

'That copper from Scotland Yard and his friend with the glasses. I know their sort. Terrorise you into admitting something you haven't done.'

I didn't tell her that the 'pig' she spoke of was my brother. I was afraid of alienating her even more. 'That won't happen whilst I'm here,' I promised. 'But Verity, if you did know something, it would be much easier if you told me. We can only clear Clyde's name if we can speak to him.'

'That's what they always say, and

then an innocent person gets hung. It's not right.'

'I hope you know me better than that.'

'It's not up to you, though, is it? Not now that they're in charge.'

'Then help me to help you, Verity. If I can say you've been co-operative, no one need be hung . . . hanged.'

'I honestly don't know,' she insisted. 'He hasn't been in touch with me.' She lowered her voice. 'He might have talked to his mother, though.'

'His mother? I don't think I know Mrs Smith.'

'Yes you do, but I don't think she's called Mrs Smith really. It's Pearl.'

'Pearl? Town-hall-steps Pearl? She's Clyde's mother?'

Verity nodded.

The 'town hall steps' was a euphemism for where the local prostitutes congregated, usually on a Friday night, when everyone was paid. They didn't actually stand on the steps in front of the town hall; they frequented the narrow alley behind it, called Butchers' Lane. Since the year 2000, that alley has become filled with trendy boutiques, holistic healers, Fair Trade stores, and bistro-style coffee shops. But in the '60s it was as the name said, where most of the butchers' shops stood, along with a couple of tatty barbers' shops that offered 'something for the weekend' (this could mean anything from contraceptives to drugs), and an equally tatty newsagent's that allowed the women to put cards in the window offering 'massages' and escort services.

As for the women working in the alley, every now and then we had a 'clean-up' to show we were doing our job. But for the most part we left them alone, and they left the rest of Stony End alone, staying away from the more public areas. Despite my role, and the fact that I did not really approve of the women's occupation, it was hard not to become familiar and almost on friendly terms with them. As the years went on and I matured, I judged their choices less, understanding how easily one bit of bad luck could lead a woman down that path.

Pearl was their undisputed leader. She looked after the women and made sure the pimps kept away. She also sent underage girls packing, telling them there was no place for them there. But other than that, I knew very little about her. I didn't even know where she lived. She always said she had no fixed abode when we arrested her, and that she had no family, until Verity told me about Clyde.

'I'll speak to her,' I said, just as the cell door opened and my brother and his friend appeared.

'You're here, Bobbie,' said Tom, his eyes narrowing. 'Has she said anything?'

'No,' I lied. 'She doesn't know anything, Tom. Why don't you just let her go?'

'Do you know about her record?' Tom asked, waving a file in front of my face. 'Shoplifting, breaking and entering at her boarding house last year . . . '

'She had a good reason for that.'

'Soliciting.'

'What?' I looked across to Verity, who was busy studying her feet. I knew that Pearl had sent her packing from the town hall steps, but I thought that had been enough to put Verity off.

'I wasn't going to do anything,' she said, tears filling her eyes. 'It was when I was homeless in London. I was desperate. But until they arrested me, I kept turning blokes down. Honestly.'

'That's what they all say,' said Tom.

'It's OK, Verity,' I soothed, shooting a sharp glance at my brother. 'Everyone makes mistakes.'

I followed my brother and Carl from the cell, locking it behind me. 'You're not going to tell her bosses, are you, Tom?' I asked my brother. 'Verity has turned her life around. She's a good kid.'

'It depends how co-operative she can be,' he said. 'But we've got bigger fish to fry at the moment. Mr Preston is awake, so we're off to the hospital to speak to him. You can come, if you want in on this investigation. Carl seems to think we should let you. We'll leave Miss Foster to consider her options.'

I let my brother and Carl go ahead, and as I was leaving the station, I saw the sarge. 'Sarge,' I said, glancing towards the cells, 'about Verity . . . '

'Don't worry, Blandford. I'll sort it out. Your brother isn't the boss here yet.'

I checked to see that my brother was out of earshot. 'When I get back, I need to go and speak to Pearl. Did you know she was Clyde's mother?'

The sarge shrugged and shook his head. 'No idea, but good call. I take it you've not mentioned it to Scotland Yard.'

'No, they'd bring everyone on Butchers' Lane in. It's odd, Sarge — you think you know someone, but suddenly you don't. I've looked up to Tom for years, and I still love him as my brother.

I just don't know if I like the person he has become. My Tom would never have talked down to Verity the way he just did.' I blushed, unsure why I was laying out my heart to the sarge. Alf was my usual shoulder to cry on when Annabel wasn't around. I waited for an acerbic reply.

'It's not about your brother, Blandford. It would be the same whoever came from Scotland Yard. They have their new systems and strategies, and in a big sprawling place like London those systems work. No one knows each other down there, so people are isolated and easier to bully into giving up information. The Scotland Yard blokes soon find out it's a bit different in the country, where people stick up for each other a bit more. As for Tom, don't be too hard on him. I just think he's a young man with a lot to prove.'

'Yes, maybe you're right, Sarge.' I tried to hide my amazement. I'd never heard the sarge say so much, unless he was telling me off.

'He reminds me of someone else who thinks they have a lot to prove,' he added. 'Must run in the family.'

'Ah, there you are, Sarge,' I said with a smile. 'I thought we'd lost you for a minute there.'

'Now don't get cheeky, Blandford.' His eyes gleamed. 'Get on with you. Scotland Yard is waiting.'

The sarge might sometimes be irascible, and I admit I was occasionally scared of him. But in that moment we were united in our wish for Stony End station to run an investigation in its own way.

The local hospital was about three miles from Stony End, just outside the next big town. It was a sprawling Victorian building that had once been a workhouse. On a dull day it still had that stark look, and you could almost imagine shoeless urchins coming from it, singing about all the glorious food they would love to eat. Inside, the pale green walls and tiled floors did nothing to cheer the building up. Damp emanated from the ceiling, due to a roof that was always leaking, and there was that slightly sour antiseptic smell you could only associate with a hospital. But it was spotlessly clean in a way few hospital wards are nowadays. Patients lay in long wards that had at least ten beds on either side, their only privacy the green curtains surrounding each bed. There were very strict rules about visiting times, enforced by a matron, who made sure no relatives sat by a bed chatting until late into the night, even if someone was critically ill.

We were allowed to take liberties, within reason. We were the police, and there was occupational camaraderie between us and the medical staff. There's a reason nurses often marry policemen. Their lives overlap on a regular basis.

I don't think anyone was prepared for my brother that day. Tom breezed into the ward without explanation, quickly identifying Mr Preston's bed and pulling up a chair. Carl and I could only follow, standing at the end of the bed. Mr Preston lay there, ashen-faced, and still slightly confused.

'Mr Preston,' said Tom, 'I'm Detective Blandford. I'm looking into the bank robbery. What can you tell us about what happened?'

'I don't . . . I can't . . . '

'Is there any sign of amnesia? Carl, check the patient record.'

Carl did as he was bid, at which point a voice rang out: 'What's going on here?' It was not the matron. It was Annabel. Her blonde hair was swept back tightly into a bun, and she wore glasses. I knew that she didn't really need them. She wore them hoping it would make her seem older and more efficient amongst the male doctors. She was still stunningly beautiful, and I heard both Tom and Carl draw their breath when she appeared. 'Why are you bothering this patient?'

Tom stood up. 'I'm in charge of the investigation into the bank robbery, and I need to speak to Mr Preston.'

'Then you should have come to me

first,' said Annabel. 'You can't just come in here, upsetting patients. Bobbie, you should know better.'

I blushed down to my toes. 'I'm sorry, Annabel. It's just that Tom . . . '

'Tom? Your brother Tom? What about him?'

'That would be me,' said Tom.

'Really?' Annabel looked him up and down. 'Good manners obviously don't run in the family.'

'And how do you know my family?'

'She's my landlady and my friend,' I muttered, wishing I could crawl under Mr Preston's bed. Tom was definitely making his presence known.

'This is Annabel? The duke's daughter? I ought to have known.' Tom's lips curled in a half-smile. 'I need to speak to this patient, Dr North. We have an ongoing investigation.'

'I appreciate that,' said Annabel. 'But you should have asked for permission before storming in here and disturbing him. I could have prepared him for your arrival. Now I'm going to have to ask you to leave.' As she spoke, Annabel checked Mr Preston's pulse. Her brow furrowed, showing how worried she was about him.

'Is there anyone . . . senior I can speak to?' asked Tom.

'You mean male, don't you?' Annabel raised an eyebrow. 'Not really. I'm in charge of this ward this afternoon. If you want to make an appointment to see Mr Preston, we'll sort it out; but for now, he needs his rest.'

'If you insist on being difficult,' Tom said, 'we'll come back tomorrow at two o'clock.' He stormed from the ward, followed by Carl.

'Annabel,' I said as I watched them go, 'I'm sorry. I know he's my brother, but I'm the junior here.'

'It's OK, Bobbie. But really, I always thought your brother was nice.'

'He is. I mean, normally.'

'Hmmph. Honestly, sweetie, I know he's your brother, but he's the most arrogant man I've ever met.'

When I got outside, Tom was waiting

by the car, smoking a cigarette. Carl was sitting at the wheel, waiting for us. 'So that's your landlady,' my brother said.

'Yes, she is, and she's my best friend.'

'I don't know how you put up with her. She's bloody impossible!'

7

Anyone who has ever read a romantic novel could see where things between Annabel and Tom were leading. I obviously hadn't read enough of them. All I could see was that my best friend and my brother hated each other with a passion, and it made me desperately unhappy.

To be honest, I couldn't blame anyone for not liking Tom those first few days after he arrived in Stony End. He burst upon us like a one-man army, making us feel like failures for our style of policing, and riding roughshod over people's feelings, whether they were fellow officers or members of the public.

I had grown up hero-worshipping my big brother. He had always looked after me, seeing off any bullies who dared try to intimidate me. He became a big brother to my friends too. When one girl came to our house crying because her boyfriend had dumped her, Tom made her a cup of tea and told her that she was far too nice for the boyfriend anyway. She went away smiling, and probably a little bit in love. Tom made sure he was always on the right side of appropriate, and never took advantage of any of the girls who came to cry on my shoulder, but they always left feeling a lot better about themselves after he had spoken to them.

When he left to go to Henley, he was full of ideals about protecting the innocent and catching the guilty, just as I was when I joined the police force. But something had changed him. He'd become abrupt and unfeeling. I don't think it was entirely about him having something to prove. I became certain that something had happened to make him that way, but I was so annoyed and embarrassed by him in those first days, I wasn't in the mood to try to find out.

When we returned to Stony End, it was too early for me to go and see

Pearl. The women on the town hall steps wouldn't come out till much later. Instead I went to see my friend, Mrs Higgins. Her garden had been gone over by the police to ensure no more evidence had been left by the bank robbers. If I didn't know better, I'd say that she sometimes claimed her land had been trespassed on as a way of getting her vegetable patch dug for her. Nothing else had been found, but it did beg the question of why the leader of the robbers had dumped the mask there. The land led to a small copse, which itself led to the Peaks and Little Stony, if one were willing to cross the fields and traverse a rather steep cliff face. Sometimes sheep got stuck on the ledges, so it was not beyond the realms of possibility that a human being could climb it.

'I hear your brother is making waves,' said Mrs Higgins as she poured me a cup of tea and cut me a slice of date and walnut cake, which she liberally smeared with butter. We were sitting at the dinette in her compact caravan, where she managed to keep everything in its place. Mrs Higgins might look a mess, usually due to her strange choice of clothing, but her home was not.

I'd given up working out the mystery of how gossip travelled in Stony End, but sometimes I left the station, having only just received a call out, only for half a dozen people on the way to tell me what had happened.

'I don't know what's happened to him,' I said. 'He never used to be like that.'

'It'll be a woman.'

'I don't think he has time for a love life,' I said. 'I barely have time myself nowadays.'

'Hmm, it's a sad thing, Dr Stanhope not supporting his brother. Or you, for that matter.'

'How on earth . . . ?' I put up my hand. 'No, don't tell me how you know about that.' I sipped my tea and took a bite of date and walnut cake. Immediately I felt calmer. Some people drink. Some people take drugs. Some people do yoga. For me, cake was the universal treatment for stress, and I was lucky in that Mrs Higgins and Greta Norris were both unashamed dealers in cakey goodness. 'Tom didn't used to be like that,' I repeated, as much to convince myself as Mrs Higgins. I told her about our childhood and how kind he could be. I knew I was making excuses for him, but I hated that people disliked my brother. I still loved him.

'He doesn't get enough cake, if you ask me,' said Mrs Higgins.

'He probably doesn't have anyone to make it for him.'

'I'll make him one,' she said. 'What does he like best?'

'Bakewell pudding.'

'Bakewell pudding it is then.'

'Not tart.'

'Certainly not.' It's a little-known fact that Bakewell puddings and tarts are very different confections. Even today, if someone goes into a pudding shop in Bakewell to ask for a 'tart', they'll be told in no uncertain terms that there aren't any tarts in Bakewell.

'What do you know about Pearl?' I asked Mrs Higgins when we had sorted out the business of my brother's cake, which had led to more reminiscences about my childhood. Odd how I trusted her with that information, knowing how easily she picked up gossip. Sometimes I wonder if she put something in the date and walnut cake.

'Town-hall-steps Pearl?'

'Yes, that's the one.'

'Only what everyone else knows.'

'Did you know that Clyde Smith was her son?' I probed.

'Oh yes. His father was an African prince.'

I wondered if this was Mrs Higgins's fantasy, or Pearl's. 'I thought he was from the West Indies.'

'The princes were all taken over there as slaves, weren't they?'

I couldn't dispute that possibility. 'I didn't even know Pearl had a family.'

'She's had a few kids. Understandable in that line of business. When I was in the resistance, seducing Nazis for information, we knew how to prevent such things. Did you know that the new contraceptive pill was developed years ago, but the Catholic Church blew up all the factories and blamed the war?'

'Right . . . ' I was pretty sure that was not true. 'So back to Pearl. Do you know any of her other children? Clyde might have gone to one of them.'

'No, he won't have done that. He's the eldest. I think the others are all in care homes.'

'That's sad.'

'Yes . . . ' Mrs Higgins had a faraway look. 'No mother gets over having her children snatched from her loving arms. Even given what Pearl is, she wasn't a bad mother.'

'How do you know?'

'I don't know. Who said I knew? Why would I know?'

'You said it as if you knew for certain.'

'And you trust my word at all times, do you, young Bobbie?' Mrs Higgins winked, but I had the distinct feeling I was being distracted.

'What do you know about Mr Preston?' I asked, deciding to do my own bit of diverting. The problem with Mrs Higgins was that once she went off on a flight of fancy, it was hard to bring her down to earth. Changing the subject sometimes brought her back to the point.

'He lives on the Stockport road in a bungalow. They call it the Ponderosa. Like the *Bonanza* ranch. Or is it *Rawhide?*' Despite her low-level living, Mrs Higgins managed to own a television and was an avid viewer.

'*Bonanza*, I think. That's him and his cousin, Mr Otterburn?'

'Yes. Mr Otterburn is an artist. He's got some very nice paintings in that gallery in the big town. But he made his living drawing those smutty postcards. You know the sort — ladies with big bosoms and fat men looking for their little Willy.'

I laughed. 'I know what you mean.'

It's odd how you don't consider that someone actually makes a living creating such cards. They're such a staple of every seaside town that one imagines they grow there in the racks, magically reproducing whenever they're close to selling out. 'What else do you know about them?'

'They're both widowed,' said Mrs Higgins. She stood up, bustling about tidying up the tea things.

'And?' I said, sensing that she was feeling uncomfortable.

'And nothing. They're two elderly gentlemen who share a house. It happens all over, doesn't it? Like you and Dr North sharing a house. Except you're not elderly men.'

'Well, yes.'

In more modern times, lodgers are a rarity. Families have become used to having their home to themselves, and there are more flats (or apartments as we're now expected to call them) for single people. In 1962, with rationing still within living memory, lots of people let out their spare room. And it was not unusual for two people who had lost family during the war to combine their financial resources, as Mrs Marrick and Miss Hooper had. I came to the conclusion that Mr Preston and Mr Otterburn did the same, but I could not understand why Mrs Higgins felt so uncomfortable talking about it. You may think me naive, but it was a more innocent time, and we did not automatically jump to conclusions about people.

'Is there something you're not telling me?' I asked.

'No, nothing.'

Realising that Mrs Higgins had told me all she was willing to say, I got up to leave. 'Thank you for the tea and cake,' I said.

'You're welcome, as always, dear,' she said with a smile. 'It's nice to have someone to talk to. I'll do your brother's cake and send it along to the station.'

It was getting dark when I stepped down out of the caravan, so I immediately noticed the light coming from the shed at the end of her garden. It was an old brick building that she used as a bathhouse. The way the light moved suggested that whoever was in there had a torch.

'Someone's there,' I said.

'No, surely not,' she insisted.

I was already halfway up the path. 'Bobbie, there's no one there,' Mrs Higgins said.

Ignoring her, I pushed open the door of the shed. I couldn't see anyone, but I could hear heavy breathing. I took out my own torch and shone it around the room. There was a makeshift bed in one corner. Then the light caught the big tin bath that was lying upside down on the floor. I put my hand on the handle and tipped it over, to reveal the figure lying there.

He jumped up and made to run past me, but Mrs Higgins stopped him. 'It's too late, lad. She's seen you. Time to face up to it, I think.'

I could hardly believe what I was seeing. 'Clyde?'

8

Throughout his interrogation, Clyde Smith insisted that Mrs Higgins had not known he was in the outhouse. I could see that Tom and Carl did not believe him, and to be honest, neither did I.

'How could you?' I said to her as she waited at the station. 'Why didn't you trust me?'

'I trust you, Bobbie. But you've seen the way they've treated that boy since they brought him in.'

'Well, yes, because in hiding out in your shed, he's behaved like someone who's guilty.'

Soon afterward, Clyde's mother, Pearl, arrived at the station. She wore a thin blue silk dress and a leopard-skin fur coat, and was obviously dressed for 'work'. 'I want to see him,' she demanded.

'Of course,' I said. 'I'll go and find out when you can go in.'

I entered the interrogation room just as Tom was slamming his hand down on the table. It made me jump. 'Tell us why you were hiding. Who else was in on it with you? Where are they?'

Clyde had a dark lump near his eye. I wondered how he had got it.

'In answer to your questions,' said Clyde, 'because I'm black and my mother is on the game. No one else is in on anything. And I don't know.'

'You were seen at the bank.'

'No, I wasn't. Because I wasn't there.'

'Tom,' I said, 'Clyde's mum would like to see him.'

'Oh God,' Clyde said, starting to cry. 'Tell her to go away, Miss Blandford, please. I don't want her to see me here.'

'She's worried about you, Clyde.'

'She should be,' said Tom. 'He's about to go to prison for bank robbery.'

'Can I speak to you alone, Tom? Please?' I asked.

With some reluctance, my brother followed me outside, leaving Carl alone with Clyde. I comforted myself that at least Carl would be kind to him. I could hear him speaking softly to Clyde whilst we were outside.

'What on earth are you doing, Tom? Did you hit that boy?'

'Of course I didn't hit him.'

'Then why does he have a bruise on his face?'

'He fell and hit himself on the pavement outside the station. Or so I was told. I'm surprised you even have to ask me, Bobbie.'

'Are you, Tom? Are you really? Because since you've arrived in Stony End, you've been riding roughshod over everyone, acting like the big tough policeman, determined to solve this crime. Why shouldn't I believe that you've hit that boy?'

'I don't do that, Bobbie, and I'm hurt that you even think so. I do everything by the book.'

'His mother wants to see him. If you

do care about doing things by the book, then you have to let her. He's still a minor.'

Tom let out a big sigh. 'All right. Bring her through.'

When Pearl saw the state of Clyde, she let out a cry of despair and took him into her arms. 'Who did it, sweetheart? Which of these . . . ' She uttered an expletive questioning my brother and Carl's parentage. ' . . . hurt you?'

Clyde, who was head and shoulders taller than his mum, looked across the room at Tom. I saw the fear in his eyes and became filled with shame. 'No one, mum. I must have hurt myself when I fell.'

'We want a solicitor,' said Pearl. 'I know my rights.'

'I bet you do,' said Tom.

'Tom!' I snapped, forgetting for a moment that he was actually my superior. No matter what Pearl did for a living, we always treated her with respect.

'I apologise, Mrs Smith,' said Tom. 'Please, sit down, and we'll fetch the duty solicitor.' He went to leave the room, then turned back. 'Clyde, if you have any complaints to make about your treatment tonight, then he's the man to talk to.'

I was not sure if Tom was threatening Clyde or not. The way my brother had been acting, I would not have put it past him.

'Would you like a cup of tea, Pearl?' I asked. 'And you, Clyde?'

'Thank you, Bobbie, that would be nice,' Pearl said.

'I'll help you,' said Carl, following me to the kitchenette. I liked him for giving Pearl and Clyde time to talk.

'Thanks, Carl. In fact, could you wait for the kettle to boil? I just need to make a phone call.'

Half an hour later the duty solicitor had arrived, and just behind him was Leo, carrying his medical bag. 'Thanks for coming,' I said. 'I'd like you to take a look at Clyde Smith before they question him any further.'

Leo did not ask me why. I think my

distressed telephone call had told him all he needed to know. He went straight through to the interview room and gave Clyde a thorough medical, in the presence of Pearl and the duty solicitor. Afterwards, whilst Tom and Carl questioned Clyde, Leo came to find me. I was in the kitchenette, nursing a cold cup of tea.

'Well?' I said, looking up at him. My heart lurched when I saw his handsome face, full of concern. It sounds silly, but each time I saw him it was like the first time, and all I could do was wonder at how beautiful he was. Sometimes I felt stupidly grateful that he was mine. Then I remembered all we had been through and wondered if he ever could really be mine.

'You think someone hit him?'

'I was told that he had hit his face on the pavement outside the station.'

Leo shook his head. 'No, that's not it. I'm pretty certain he was hit with a fist.'

I put down my cup and put my head in my hands.

'Hey, hey . . . ' Leo sat next to me and put his arms around me. 'What is it, darling?'

'I think Tom did it,' I murmured against his neck. 'What do I do, Leo? Clyde won't press charges, but he should, even if it's my own brother.'

'I asked him if he wanted to press charges, but he said no. In which case, there's nothing you can do, sweetheart. But your brother knows now that I'm keeping an eye on him. I only wish I'd met Tom in better circumstances.'

'I'm sorry for getting you out.'

'You know you only have to ask for me and I'll come running.'

I smiled at him. As my love for him swelled in my chest, I forgot everything he'd said about my job not being good enough for Joe. I only knew that I could never love anyone else in the same way. I wanted to be in his arms, and for him never to go away.

'Yes, I know you do, Leo. Annabel is doing a double shift tonight. Will you wait till I've finished here and come home with me? I want . . . ' I didn't really have to tell him what I wanted. I could see by his eyes that it was what he wanted too.

He kissed me tenderly. 'Like I said, you only have to ask.'

Clyde was charged with evading arrest, but they had no real proof he had been involved in the bank robbery, apart from Mrs Ogden's testimony, which was not perfect. Even the Frank Sinatra mask found in Mrs Higgins's garden was not proof, as Mrs Ogden had said that Clyde had been wearing the Sammy Davis Jr mask.

Later that night, or early into the next morning to be exact, I got out of bed, leaving Leo sleeping, and went to the window. Something had disturbed me, but I did not know what. Annabel's cottage was on a quiet street that did not have much in the way of street lighting. I looked out and felt sure there was a figure standing across the road.

A match flared, as if someone were lighting a cigarette. It only briefly illuminated part of the man's face, which was shaded by a hat, but it was far too quick for me to see who it was. He turned and walked away. I told myself it was probably someone who was out for a late-night walk, but something about the way the man seemed to be looking in the direction of Annabel's cottage unnerved me.

'What is it?' asked Leo, stirring as if he had sensed my unease.

'Nothing,' I said. I got back into bed and sank into the comfort of his arms. 'I'm just seeing shadows where there are none. Hold me tight and everything will be all right again.'

9

I don't want to give the impression that the Stony End police were doing nothing about the bank robbery until my brother and his friend came up from Scotland Yard. We had been making house-to-house enquiries, asking who might have seen anything. We questioned everyone who worked at the bank, and everyone who had been in and around it when the robbery took place.

What we knew was that there had been four robbers. Despite their masks, two of them had given the impression of being older men, and the other two were apparently younger. One of the younger men might have been black, but as Mrs Ogden was the only one saying that, it was not entirely certain. Other witnesses had not seen enough of the men to be sure. They had been seen escaping in a van, but the witnesses differed on whether it was navy-blue or black, with one witness even insisting it was brown.

One morning I went out with Alf in the Zephyr, and we tested whether it was possible that Clyde could have taken part in the robbery, and then been able to get to the cash and carry, then return to Mr Patel's shop in the grocery van — full of new goods — before Miller and I got there.

'It would be tight,' Alf said. 'But he could have done it if he'd gone to the cash and carry earlier, then left Mr Patel's van hidden somewhere.'

'It's too complicated a plan,' I said. 'Why, if he had all that money from the bank robbery, would he bother going back to Mr Patel's?'

'Maybe Patel was involved. Perhaps he launders the money through his rental properties.' When Alf saw my angry expression, he threw up his hands in supplication. 'We have to think of every possibility, lass, even if it's not what we want to believe. You know that.'

'I don't believe it. These bank robberies have happened all over the country. Mr Patel gave us his order book with a list of deliveries. We checked with everyone that Clyde was the one who delivered the groceries on those days. He couldn't be in Stony End and Dartford or Manchester at the same time. Mrs Ogden was wrong about him. She's one of those people who don't like black men, so she created one as a villain in the robbery, and now Clyde is under suspicion for no other reason than his colour.'

'I don't disagree with you, lass. I'm just reminding you to keep an open mind.'

We also searched for a base of operations from which the bank robbers might have worked. We finally found a house that might be a possibility, but it was after Tom and Carl arrived, so they insisted on coming with Alf and me to check it out. It was a derelict cottage about five miles from Stony End, and the nearest neighbour, Mr Bennett, had reported seeing lights flickering.

'No one's lived there for years,' said Mr Bennett. He and his wife had a smallholding about a mile across the fields from the derelict cottage. 'Sometimes kids go up there to smoke and drink, or if it's a boy and a girl they go to neck I suppose, but they only stay a couple of hours. I noticed that lights were on in the place for a day or two.'

'Why didn't you report it sooner?' asked Tom, sounding harsher than necessary.

'I didn't think anything about it at the time. For all I knew, they'd finally sold the place. Then we had to go away the night before the bank robbery to stay with my sister in Derby, as she's been poorly. Unfortunately she died while we were there, and we had to stay and sort out her funeral. I didn't hear about what happened till I got back.'

'It was in all the papers,' Tom said.

'I'd just lost my sister, so I wasn't really keeping up with the news.'

'Thank you, Mr Bennett,' I cut in,

glaring at Tom. 'It might be nothing, but we'll check it out.'

We thought we would have to leave our vehicles on the road and trudge through the fields, but it seemed that someone had cleared a path to the derelict cottage, and there were signs that cars or vans had recently used that path.

As Alf and Carl went ahead, I grabbed my brother by the arm. 'What is your problem, Tom?'

'What do you mean?'

'That poor man has lost his sister, and you snap his head off for not reading the newspapers? What's happened to you? You didn't used to be like this.'

'Look, Bobbie, there are things going on that I can't tell you about.'

'And this justifies treating valuable witnesses and vulnerable boys like they're dirt?'

Tom's nostrils flared, and I could see the muscle in his jaw working. 'Bobbie, just remember something. I'm the senior officer here. You're only just out of probation. And you're in the women's service at that. So don't tell me how to do my job!'

'Well that told me, didn't it?' I snapped. It reminded me of Leo saying that policing was not good enough for his brother, Joe. I stormed on ahead, trying not to lose control of my emotions.

'Bobbie . . . I . . . ' Tom called. He said something that might have been an apology, and then something else about me understanding one day, but I was in no mood to listen.

When I reached the cottage, only Carl had gone inside. Alf had gone to look around the perimeter. 'Are you OK, Bobbie?' Carl asked.

'No, not really. To be honest, I'm sick of having to prove myself — first to Leo, and now to Tom. Everyone underestimates me.'

'Well, I don't. I've heard good things from Alf about the work you do at Stony End station.'

'Thanks,' I said, slightly mollified.

'Anyway, sorry, none of this is your problem.'

'I'm always happy to listen. My shoulders can cope with a bit of crying on.'

I laughed at that. 'Thanks again. Let's look around, shall we?'

The cottage showed definite signs of occupation. There were empty tins of Irish stew and Heinz beans strewn over a table, along with some newspapers from the days after the bank robbery. The outside toilet had also been used recently, and was blocked.

'They were here for a couple of days afterwards,' I said, looking at the dates on the newspapers, all of which reported the robbery. By that time, Tom and Alf had joined us. 'So if Clyde was in on it, why didn't he come here? Why go hide in Mrs Higgins's shed?' I gave my brother a pointed look.

'He was probably afraid to lead us to them,' said Tom.

'Yes, that's probably right, Bobbie,' said Carl apologetically.

'No, I'm not buying that. If he was in

on it, and had some of the money, he wouldn't have hung around Stony End.'

'Maybe they stiffed him on it,' said Tom. 'It's been done before. I know you like the kid, Bobbie, but that doesn't mean he's not guilty.'

'And just because you don't like him, or the colour of his skin, doesn't mean he *is* guilty.' I had never felt ashamed of my brother before, but I was beginning to.

'Bobbie, it's nothing to do with his skin tone . . .'

'Right,' said Alf, clapping his hands together as if they were cold. 'Let's not get into this now, shall we? Let's stick to the matter in hand . . . sir,' he added for Tom's benefit.

I left them in the main room of the cottage and went upstairs. The dust on the floor had been unsettled, suggesting that the gang had been sleeping on it. There were more newspapers, used to cover up the windows. They were much older. The date said April 1944. I almost missed it, then realised that there was a front page with the story of an earlier bank robbery in Stony End. The details were scant, mainly because the war took up most of the front page, but it said that one of the clerks had been injured and hospitalised.

I went back downstairs to tell the others. Only my brother and Alf were there. 'Where's Carl?' I asked.

'He's gone back to the car to radio and ask forensics to come out and look for fingerprints.'

'Oh. Right. It might be a coincidence, but I think it's the same gang that carried out the robbery in the war. It seems they like to read about their crimes.' I explained about the newspapers in the windows upstairs. 'Someone's been sleeping up there too.'

'Sounds like it. Good find, sis,' said Tom. My eyes narrowed. I really did not need him patronising me.

'You'll probably find something about the earlier robbery in your vault, Bobbie,' said Alf.

'Yes, maybe.'

'Vault?' Tom looked at us quizzically.

'It's the cellar at the station. I have all the old cold cases down there,' I said.

'Bobbie's helped solve a lot of cases by looking at the old stuff,' said Alf. I loved my friend and mentor for sticking up for me.

'I'd be interested in seeing it,' said Tom.

I turned away from him, determined not to be swayed by his attempt to mollify me. If I was to find out the truth about my brother's behaviour, I knew I had to be tough. Even if it broke my heart to see how much he had changed.

Carl returned from the car, and we continued to make notes about what we had found in the cottage. There were the newspapers, charting both crimes, and lots of tins and jars off which we might be able to get fingerprints.

'Look at this,' Alf said, holding up a jar that had held orange marmalade. 'It was bought in the market, from Mrs Marrick's stall.'

'I could go to see her and ask if she

remembers selling it,' I suggested.

'Constable Norris,' said Tom, 'will you stay here until forensics arrives, please? We don't want anyone coming along and upsetting this lot.'

'Yes, sir,' Alf agreed.

'Bobbie, why don't you go with Carl to interview Mrs Green and Mrs Ogden again? They might feel more comfortable with a WPC present.'

I almost pointed out that he hadn't been that thoughtful when questioning Verity Foster, but I bit my tongue. At least whilst I was around, I could make sure that Tom did not cross the line. 'What about Mrs Marrick?' I asked.

'You can speak to her some other time. I want you to do this now.'

'Yes, sir,' I said, sounding churlish even to myself.

'What are you going to do?' Carl asked Tom.

'I'm going over to Sheffield, so see if the local plods can find a place like this nearby, where the thieves holed up. That way we may be able to definitely connect the two robberies.'

'Why would they need another place?' I asked. 'They can reach Sheffield from here.'

'True,' said Tom. 'But there are no newspapers here about that robbery.'

I had to admit he had a point, but I suspected that he was up to something else.

*   *   *

'Sorry you got stuck with me,' I said to Carl as we drove back toward Stony End.

'I don't mind at all, Bobbie. I think women have a lot to offer the police service. More so than men. We sometimes lack empathy, but you obviously have tons of it.'

I smiled gratefully. 'I'm glad someone sees my worth.'

'Trouble with the boyfriend, eh?' I don't know if I imagined it, but he seemed hopeful.

'No. I mean, not really. We've had our

ups and downs, but we always get through them.'

'What are you going to do if there are more downs than ups, Bobbie? Sometimes it's best to just walk away if being with someone makes you unhappy.'

'Leo doesn't make me unhappy. Sometimes the situations we get into make me unhappy. But . . . ' I floundered. Carl had hit the nail on the head. Leo and I had definitely had more downs than ups in our relationship. Sometimes it felt like hard work, trying to fit our romance into our careers. Then there was the time when I found out he had married a woman in Las Vegas. It all turned out all right in the end, but now I was not so sure. We had been OK again since Leo made his remark about policing not being good enough for Joe, but was being OK enough?

'Well, you can always talk to me,' Carl said. 'Just as friends.'

'Thank you. But I've said enough.' I should not have been discussing our relationship with a virtual stranger. I could not fight the feeling that I had been disloyal to Leo. Carl was so easy to talk to, and at least he appreciated my worth.

Not that I was romantically interested in Carl. It was just that after Leo and my brother, who were both alpha males, it made a change to be around a beta male who asked nothing of me and did not make me feel that I had to prove myself.

'Oh, we're here,' I said, as we turned into the street where Mrs Green and Mrs Ogden lived. It turned out they were neighbours, living in adjoining terraced railway cottages opposite the train station. It was interesting to note that their houses were almost carbon copies of each other. They had the same net curtains and the same colour of front door. They even had the same flowers in the tiny front gardens.

Inside was more of a mirror image, as many of those cottages are. But even their furniture was the same: G-Plan three-piece suites, with Nottingham lace antimacassars over the arms and the backs of the sofa and both chairs. A fold-up teak dining table was placed under the front window, with a chair either side (I guessed that the other chairs were in the bedroom, and only brought down on special occasions — my mother had done exactly the same), and the galley kitchens had the same blue and white units. I could not help wondering who was keeping up with whom. The only difference was that Mrs Green had a brand-new Electrolux cooker, and Mrs Ogden had an old coal-fired range.

We saw Mrs Green first. She lived with her husband, Len, and their Labrador, Bob. He was a gorgeous dog, who made a huge fuss of me. Mr Green was the strong, silent type, who only grunted when his wife spoke to him. He was watching *Grandstand* on the television, and it took his wife some coaxing to make him turn it down so that we could speak.

'Z-Cars is on in a bit,' said Mr Green. 'So I hope you're not going to take too long.'

Z-Cars would not be on for another three or four hours, but I did not say so. 'It's not very true to life anyway,' I said mischievously. Actually, Annabel and I were big fans of the show. It starred Brian Blessed as Fancy Smith, and though it's hard to believe, he didn't shout at people all the time back then.

'We just need to ask you a few more questions,' said Carl.

'Let me make a cup of tea,' Mrs Green said. She was dressed in a blue pinafore, fussing around plumping up cushions in an attempt to straighten up a room that was already straightened to perfection.

'There's no need to go to any trouble,' I said. 'We just need to ask if you've thought of anything else that might help us.' Sometimes when the shock wore off, witnesses did remember more. Occasionally they remembered things that had not happened, but that

117

was a risk we had to take.

Mrs Green gestured for us to sit down on the sofa. Unfortunately it was a fairly slippery piece of furniture, and Carl and I found ourselves sliding close together. I struggled to sit up straight, as Bob (the dog!) put his head on my knee. It was difficult to behave professionally in such conditions.

'I've already answered lots of questions,' said Mrs Green. 'You don't think I had anything to do with it, did you?'

'Not at all,' Carl said disarmingly. 'Can you take us through again what happened on that day?'

'Well, it was a normal Friday. We knew that the van from Mappings would be coming to collect the wages. Mr Preston — bless that dear man — was waiting for them. It was just a normal Friday,' she repeated. 'Then they came in. Wearing their masks. They had guns. I don't know what sort. Everyone screamed, and the leader shouted at them all to be quiet. Mr Preston came from the back room, and the leader grabbed him and asked him for the combination to the safe. Mr Preston was so brave. He refused. So the man — the one with the Frank Sinatra mask — hit him over the head. At the same time, the other men were demanding we give them money from the drawers.'

'Was there much in the drawers?' asked Carl.

'Well, yes. Friday is a busy day due to the market, so the bank always has extra money for shoppers and the like.'

'Can you tell us anything about the men in the masks that might help us?' I asked. 'Mrs Ogden said she thought one was black.'

'Oh, I'm not sure about that. Not that I want to contradict her. I'm sure if she says he was, then he was.'

'Could it have been Clyde Smith?' asked Carl.

'I really don't know,' said Mrs Green. 'I . . . well, maybe it was. He's the only one of that . . . that colour around here. I know I was sure that two of the men were middle-aged, and the other two were young. It was the way they moved and dressed, if that makes any sense.'

'Perfect sense,' I said encouragingly.

'You say that Mr Ives, the manager, was away due to his wife being in hospital,' Carl said. 'So that left Mr Preston in charge.'

'That's correct.'

'Who knew this?'

'I've no idea.'

'And you say that no one else but Mr Ives and Mr Preston knew the combination to the safe.'

'That's correct. The robbers forced Mr Preston to give it to them. Poor man . . . '

'How long have you worked at the bank, Mrs Green?' I asked.

'Oh, about ten years now, isn't it, dear?' She looked to her husband for confirmation.

'Hmmph,' he replied, looking at the carriage clock on the mantelpiece and then at the television. We had been there less than half an hour.

'So you weren't there when the last

robbery took place during the war?'

'Oh, no. We didn't live in Stony End then. We're from Stockport originally.'

'Has anyone ever told you anything about it?' I pressed her.

'Well, Mrs Ogden has mentioned it once or twice.'

'She worked there then?'

Mrs Green hesitated. 'I'm sure she had nothing to do with it.'

'No, I'm sure she didn't,' said Carl. 'We're just looking into the possibility that it was the same people.'

'Mrs Green,' I said, trying to be delicate, 'I was told that Mr Preston was very upset about you looking at his diary — '

'I didn't look at it,' she replied hotly. 'I only found it on the floor and picked it up. Then he saw me with it and gave me a telling-off.'

'So you didn't see anything in it about the day of the robbery?' asked Carl.

'No, I certainly did not.'

We spoke to Mrs Green a little while longer, but there was not much more she could tell us.

'What are you thinking?' I asked Carl as we made our way to Mrs Ogden next door. 'That it was an inside job?'

'Yes, it seems that way.'

'But who? Mr Preston was injured, and Mr Ives was off due to his wife being run over.'

'It's a scary thing, having a loved one hurt,' said Carl.

'You think they forced Mr Ives to give up the combination by threatening his wife? That's astounding.'

'Something like that.'

The more I thought about it, the more I wondered if Carl was right. I know I felt ridiculously pleased that he was sharing his theory with me. Not like Miller, who always kept me out of the loop.

We were standing on the street, and I noticed that Carl was looking at my hair. 'What's wrong?' I asked.

'Oh, sorry. There's something in your hair. A fly, I think . . . ' He leaned in and picked at something on my hair, but the button on his sleeve became caught in it. We wrestled for a couple of minutes, with his face very close to mine, as we fought my hair free from his sleeve.

When we were free of entanglement, I laughed. 'Well *that* went wrong quickly.'

I turned, still laughing, and saw Leo across the road, next to the train station. He had a serious look on his face. I waved, but he did not wave back. He just turned and went into the station.

I didn't have time to think about it, so we went to Mrs Ogden's. As I said before, the houses were mirror images of each other, even down to the folded table under the front window and the antimacassars on the G-Plan furniture.

As we walked in, a Labrador ran out of the kitchen and came to greet me. 'Get down, Bob,' said Mrs Ogden.

'Bob?' I raised an eyebrow. 'Isn't that the name of Mrs Green's dog?'

'Is it, dear? Oh yes, I remember now. What a coincidence.'

Not much of a coincidence, I

thought, considering Mrs Green's dog was obviously older than Mrs Ogden's.

Whereas next door Mr Green had sat on the chair by the fire, staring at the television, in Mrs Ogden's it was a young man in his twenties. He was wearing blue jeans and a white shirt with sleeves folded, showing off several tattoos. His greasy hair was slicked back in a Teddy Boy style, with his fringe twisted over his forehead. He was rolling a cigarette.

'Hello, Jimmy,' I said. 'How are you?' Jimmy was a regular at the station, usually on a Saturday night when he had spent all his dole money at the pub.

'Not bad, WPC Blandford. Not bad.'

'Mrs Ogden,' said Carl after we had gone through the obligatory offers of tea and a seat (also slippery), 'we wondered if we could ask you some more questions about the bank robbery.'

'I don't know much more than I've already told you,' she said, sitting on the arm of her son's chair. He nudged her and she moved quickly, going to sit on one of the dining chairs instead.

'Can you take us through it, exactly as you remember?' I said.

'Well . . . It was a normal Friday morning . . . ' She went through much the same as Mrs Green had, about them waiting for the Mappings van to come for the wages . . . they always came on a Friday . . . it was a market day so the bank was busy. This was another drawback of waiting to ask more questions. People spoke to each other and found a common story. Not deliberately, but by osmosis. It might seem obvious that people would tell the same story, but that was not the case. People saw things in terms of their own lives and their own considerations at the time, so they would throw in different observations. For example, one might have been thinking about buying fish for supper, whilst another was concerned with whether or not they'd given a customer the wrong money.

But Mrs Ogden's story was exactly the same as Mrs Green's. Just as her house was exactly the same and her dog was also called Bob. She was even wearing the same blue pinafore. Mrs Ogden seemed to have no original ideas of her own at all.

'Tell us again about the masks,' I asked, trying to get her onto something else. 'You say that you think one of the men was black?'

'Well, now I come to think of it, I don't think that can be true. I was probably just going by the mask. Wasn't I, Jimmy?'

'What you asking me for? I wasn't there.'

'No, of course not, duck. I mean that I've talked to you about it since, haven't I?'

Jimmy took a drag on his cigarette. 'Anyway, you said the bloke was black. That's what you told me.'

'Did I, duck? Oh well, then, I suppose he must have been.'

'It would be better if you remembered for yourself,' I said. 'Clyde Smith is in custody at the moment, and — '

'So?' said Jimmy, stubbing out his cigarette. His mother rushed to empty the ashtray. 'He's been in trouble before.'

'Not like this,' I said. 'And as your mother didn't actually see his face.'

'He's the only black boy around here.'

'Anyway,' said Carl, 'getting back to the point. Mrs Ogden, did you work at the bank during the last robbery?'

'Jimmy was only a baby then.'

'Yes, of course.'

'I mean I might have taken time off work to have him. I brought him up alone, you know. His father never came back from the war.'

'I'm very sorry,' I said.

'They don't want to know about Dad,' said Jimmy.

'Do you remember anything about the previous robbery?' I asked Mrs Ogden.

'No, not really. It was a long time ago.'

'How old are you, Jimmy?' asked Carl.

'Twenty. So I'd have had nowt to do with it either.'

'No, but it was eighteen years ago that it happened. So you can't have been off work, Mrs Ogden.'

'You're not suggesting *I* had anything to do with it?' she said, laughing, but blushing scarlet.

'No, not at all,' I said. 'We just wondered if you were in work that day.'

'I honestly don't remember.'

I would have thought she would remember someone coming into the bank with a gun — and if she had forgotten, then the recent robbery would have jogged her memory. But she was adamant she remembered nothing.

'The . . . the system has always been the same,' Mrs Ogden twittered. 'Only the manager and assistant manager know the combination to the safe.'

'Who was the manager back then?'

'It was old Mr Potter, but he's been dead for a while now.'

'And the assistant manager?'

Mrs Ogden looked at her son as if expecting him to remember for her. I was not sure, but it seemed to me that he shook his head slightly. 'I can't remember,' she said. 'Isn't that silly? I really don't know.'

We asked a few more questions, but there was nothing else Mrs Ogden could tell us. Or at least nothing she was willing to tell us.

'Do you think she had anything to do with both robberies?' I asked Carl as we drove back to the station.

'She's the common denominator at the moment. Have you noticed how she seems to have to have everything Mrs Green's got? Apart from the cooker.'

'Yes.'

'That must be expensive, with only one wage and Jimmy's dole money coming into the house.'

'I wonder if we're looking at a copycat robbery,' I said. 'I need to go and check my unsolved case files.'

'I could help you. I'd like to see your vault.'

'Oh, no, it's OK.'

'Ah, possessive, are you?' Carl teased.

'Maybe. A little bit.' The truth was

that I felt awkward about the way Leo had seen me with Carl. I knew there was nothing in it, but I did not want to give Leo any reasons to distrust me.

'You can't keep me out forever, Bobbie.'

'What?' I looked at Carl sharply, confused by his tone.

'Out of the cellar, to look at the case files.'

'Oh, I see.' But I wasn't sure that was what he meant at all.

10

I had been working on sorting out the cold case files for several years, when I had time and the sarge let me off from my normal duties, but had still not come close to putting them in proper order. At least the cellar at the station looked better than it had when I first went down there. Then it had been a jumble of boxes, full of files and old office furniture. Most of the furniture had gone to the local school and the Women's Institute. I had kept one desk and chair for myself with a telephone connection to upstairs.

I had originally piled all the files into the middle of the room, taking out a few at a time to put in order on the shelves around the edges. It was painstaking work, especially as I was tempted to read about every crime, no matter how trivial. In a place like Stony

End, most of those crimes were of the petty variety: broken windows, apple pies stolen off kitchen tables (few people in Stony End locked their doors), and children scrumping on private land. The cases went back to the turn of the century, which was when the station had first opened. Before then there had been just one village constable, and he lived in the one-bedroom cottage that formed part of the newer station.

Every time someone reported a crime, a file was opened; but often it was difficult to prove anything, so they remained open cases, even if those involved had long since died. Sometimes even the most trivial of crimes were clues to something bigger, including the theft of a bicycle that had given me a clue to a series of murders only the year before. So it was fair to say there were thousands of files, some with only one sheet of paper, and I had barely touched the surface of them. There were also quite a few unsolved murders and other serious crimes, particularly during World War II when resources had been stretched and it was all the station could do to ensure that the townspeople remained safe from bombing. One of those murders had been that of my father, Robert Blandford. Leo, who was a tearaway teenager at the time, had been arrested for that crime, but his elder sister had confessed. Even that turned out to be wrong, and she had only confessed to protect him. I had solved the case in my first year at Stony End, clearing both Leo and his sister.

Now I needed to find the file pertaining to the earlier bank robbery. I tended to have a good memory for anything I read, so I knew I had not already seen it. I started working through the files, trying not to get dragged into reading the more interesting cases.

'You've got it cosy down here.'

I was so engrossed in my reading that I had not heard Carl approaching. I almost dropped the file I was reading.

'You made me jump!' I said. 'You need to get louder shoes.'

'Sorry. Any luck?'

'Not yet.'

'That file you're holding must have been engrossing.'

'Oh yes, indeed. In 1955, Miss Cartwright up at Little Stony had her false teeth stolen off the windowsill. Whoever took them also took the cup of bleach in which she kept them. Ugh . . . Based on my previous experience with a stolen bicycle, I'm convinced that those false teeth will eventually lead us to the perpetrator of the theft of the crown jewels.'

'Are the crown jewels missing?'

'Not yet, but give it time.'

'Anyway,' he said, smiling in his disarming way, 'I'm sorry to have bothered you, but I was off to the pub for a pint and a meat pie and wondered if you'd like to come.'

'Oh thanks, Carl, but I really need to find this file. Besides, I'm meeting Leo later. So we'll probably see you at the pub if you're still there.' There, I

134

thought, I'd made it clear that Leo and I were an item, and that Carl had no real place in my life.

'Oh, right. See you later then.'

'Yeah, OK,' I said, my attention taken by another file. Alf always joked that I stepped into a different dimension when I was in the cellar. I certainly found the old case files enthralling, no matter how trivial the crimes might have been. They were a view into a different world, and sometimes, depending on how far back they went, with different values. In 1910 a farmer had been arrested for leading his cattle through a residential street between the hours of ten in the morning and four in the afternoon.

It was gone seven o'clock before I had to give up for the day. I had gone through dozens of files and still had not found the one I wanted. Sometimes it seemed that the more you wanted to find something, the more elusive it became.

I dusted myself off and went to the Cunning Woman. A sign said 'Under New Management'. The new landlord was actually a landlady. It was Dottie Riley, who used to own the chip shop. She had sold that to the Chinese couple and taken up the pub instead. Dottie was somewhere in her early fifties. She had over-bleached white-blonde hair piled high on her head in a myriad of curls, and a different low-cut blouse and tight-fitting pencil skirt for every day.

'Evening, Dottie,' I said. 'Can I have a lager and lime please? Have you seen Dr Stanhope?'

'Yes, he was in a short time ago, duck,' said Dottie. 'He was talking to that nice policeman.'

I looked around and saw Carl sitting in a corner. He raised his glass to me and beckoned me over.

'Thanks, Dottie,' I said.

'Your Tom is upsetting a lot of people,' Dottie said in a low voice. Dottie had known us when we were little, before we moved away to Chesterfield. Tom and Carl were staying in rooms above the pub.

'I know,' I said. 'I don't know what's

going on with him, Dottie.'

'He used to be such a lovely little boy. Always smiling. Now he looks like he's got the weight of the world on his shoulders.'

'He won't tell me what's wrong.'

'Do you want me to have a word? I could tell him he's not too old to put over my knee.'

They say that it takes a village to raise a child, and whilst I had been very young when we left Stony End, Tom had told me lots of tales of getting told off by neighbours for misbehaving.

'We daren't put a foot wrong,' he told me. 'If they didn't give me a thorough telling-off, it would get back to Mum and Dad and they'd do it.'

'No, please don't say anything, Dottie,' I pleaded now. 'It might only make things worse.'

'All right, I'll say nowt — but if he starts upsetting my customers, then all bets are off.'

'What happened to Leo?' I asked Carl when I went to sit down.

'He had a patient or something. I said I'd wait and tell you so that you weren't kept hanging on.'

'Oh right. I'll probably just drink this and head home.'

'No, don't go, Bobbie. Have something to eat. You look worn out. What do you want? I'll get it. It's all being paid for by the Met anyway.'

It seemed rude to run off and leave him, so I said I'd have a chicken and mushroom pie. 'Did Leo say if he was coming back?' I asked when he had brought my pie back. Normally when Leo and I met, we knew to wait for the other. Neither of our jobs allowed for us to be perfectly punctual. It was not unusual for Leo to be called away, just as it was not unusual for it to happen to me during the course of my duties, but I had a bad feeling because of the way he had looked at me before going into the train station earlier that day.

I picked at my pie and made small talk with Carl, all the time wondering when I could leave without offending him.

'Did you find the file about the previous bank robbery?' he asked.

'No, not yet. There's so much down there, it's hard to get through it all. Knowing my luck, it'll be right at the bottom of the pile.'

'That's always the way.'

'What do you know about their other robberies? Is Tom back from Sheffield yet?'

'No, not yet. He'll probably end up staying overnight.'

'Right, OK. And the other robberies?'

'Only that they're the same M.O., with the robbers wearing masks of celebrities. They seem to have gone for the Rat Pack this time, but before they've been Elvis or James Stewart.'

'Any news on where the masks were made? Because they're not exactly the sort of thing that's common, are they? So they must be made especially.'

'That's a good point,' said Carl. 'Anyway, let's forget about work for a bit. Tell me about you. Tom talks about you all the time. About how proud he is of you and what you're doing here.'

'Does he?' I frowned. 'I'm a bit worried about him, actually. He seems to be under a lot of pressure.'

'The job'll do that to you,' said Carl soothingly. 'But Tom's good at what he does.'

'Does he . . . does he get very angry with suspects?'

'A bit frustrated sometimes, maybe. But not angry.'

'I mean, you've worked with him. Would he hit a suspect?'

'Bobbie . . . ' Carl ran his hands through his hair. 'I couldn't say, really. I mean, there's a code, isn't there? We cover each other's backs.'

'Even when someone's getting hurt? I'm talking about Clyde.'

'Oh, the kid just fell on the pavement . . . I'm sure. Anyway, we've had to let him go on your sarge's orders. He'll be charged with resisting arrest, but that's until we gather more evidence.'

'Clyde is not guilty. Mr Patel has given him a solid alibi. I can't help thinking that Tom overreacted. I love my brother, but I can't condone violence towards people in our charge.'

'No, of course not. And as I said, I'm sure Tom wouldn't . . . Yes, he does get angry sometimes, but . . . if anything has happened, it hasn't been when I've been in the room.'

'OK. Look, I have to go.' I pushed my half-eaten pie away. 'Sorry for giving you the third degree. You're a good friend to Tom. I'm glad he's got you. Maybe it'll help him in the future, having your calming influence.'

'Don't go, Bobbie. I really enjoy your company.'

'Look, Carl, don't take this the wrong way. I really enjoy your company too. But I love Leo.'

'Of course. I never thought anything else.'

As I was leaving the pub, I bumped into Mrs Marrick, Miss Hooper, and a good-looking middle-aged man. 'Good evening,' I said.

'Good evening, WPC Blandford,' said

Mrs Marrick. 'This is my son, Alan, who's come to stay with us for a while.'

'It's nice to meet you, Mr Marrick.'

'How do you do,' said Alan, smiling. 'I gather I gave my mother and Miss Hooper a bit of a fright when I turned up the other day unannounced, and it resulted in you having to come all the way to Little Stony.'

Both Mrs Marrick and Miss Hooper looked mortified. Miss Hooper did her usual thing of playing with invisible worry beads.

'Oh?' I looked at the trio inquisitively.

'Alan arrived whilst we were in bed,' said Mrs Marrick. 'Then he was called away on some business and he went off, leaving the back door wide open. We had no idea till he returned today. I've given him a severe talking-to.' She did not appear to be joking.

'I'm not under arrest, I hope,' said Alan Marrick.

'We'll let you off this time, sir,' I said. 'But perhaps next time you could leave your mother a note?'

He laughed at that. 'Now why didn't I think of that?' He laughed all the way into the pub. 'A note. It's so simple.'

I could not help noticing that neither Mrs Marrick nor Miss Hooper were laughing. I could imagine them being annoyed that he had put them to some inconvenience, but there seemed to be more to it than that. Their story had changed entirely. First they thought they had been burgled. Then it was because Miss Hooper forgot to lock the door and Mrs Marrick had been searching for her bank book. Now it was because her son had turned up unannounced. But there was little I could do about it. No crime had been committed, apart from wasting our time. And on the scale of time-wasting, Miss Hooper and Miss Marrick were not quite up there with people who expected us to find their missing reading glasses or rescue kittens from trees.

When I returned home, it was to another surprise. Annabel was there, but so was Tom. They were in the sitting room, both holding a glass of wine, and chatting quite amiably. Annabel sat on a chair, with her gorgeous long legs crossed.

'I thought you were in Sheffield,' I said, kissing my brother on the cheek. I wanted to think the best of him, and to believe Carl when he had said that Tom might get impatient but he would not get violent. I pushed away the suspicion that Carl was covering for him.

'I was, then I bumped into Annabel at the train station. She kindly invited me for a drink.'

'I've got another invite,' said Annabel. 'And you and Tom must come. And Leo.'

'What's that?' Annabel and Tom must have got very friendly. It hardly seemed possible after their initial meeting.

'Mummy and Daddy have commanded me to go home for a weekend. There's no way I'm going on my own, and I've been told I can take some friends. So you can come with me for the weekend, Bobbie, and maybe Tom and Leo can join us for Saturday night dinner.'

'I don't know how to act around a duke and duchess,' I said, slumping down on the sofa. I couldn't help wondering how Tom and Annabel had got from crossing swords at the hospital to arranging dinner dates. Not that it was a real date; there would be others there. Nevertheless, I felt as if I'd turned up late to the second act of a play.

'Oh don't worry, darling,' said Annabel. 'I'll be there to help you. Where is Leo, anyway? Weren't you meeting him?'

'He got called away on a medical matter.'

'Same old, same old. Anyway, you tell him to keep that weekend free. It'll be fun. What am I saying?' Annabel grimaced. 'It will be horrendous, but at least I'll have you three with me to share the misery.'

As we chatted about the weekend at Annabel's parents' house, it began to feel as if Tom were my brother again.

He was smiling, mainly at Annabel, but I could not blame him for that. All the tension I had seen in him seemed to have disappeared.

'What happened in Sheffield?' I asked him.

'Nothing much. They've had no new leads. We need to catch these b . . . blighters, though. My guess is that they'll be planning another robbery soon. How did you and Carl get on with Mrs Green and Mrs Ogden?'

I explained what we had been told, but it all led to nothing. Despite that, something in my mind was making connections, as it always did when we had a big case, but I hadn't found the one thing that made them make sense.

When Tom left, I went to the phone and dialled Leo's number. He answered sleepily, 'Hello.'

'Hey,' I said. 'Sorry I missed you at the pub. I hope it was nothing too serious.'

'I was just about to say the same to you,' he said. His voice had an icy tone.

'What do you mean?'

'I was told you were called away on a case.'

'No . . . I've been looking at old case files, but I'd done by just after seven.'

'Your friend seemed to think you'd be gone all night.'

'My friend?'

'Yes, the bloke I saw stroking your hair earlier today. Carl?'

'He wasn't stroking my hair, Leo. He said I had a fly in it or something, then his button got caught in my hair and . . . ' It sounded ridiculous when I said it out loud. 'Nothing is happening.'

'I wouldn't have worried until you said 'nothing is happening'. Now I am worried.'

'Leo, Carl is just a friend. In fact, he's not even that. He's a colleague.'

'So you enjoyed your chicken and mushroom pie with him then?'

The old Stony End tom toms had clearly been in use. 'No, I left half of it and came home. Annabel has invited me to her father's pile for the weekend.

That's why I was ringing. To see if you wanted to come to dinner there on the Saturday night.'

'I don't know if I can get away.'

'Leo, there's nothing between me and Carl.'

'I know, Bobbie.' He sighed, sounding tired. 'Look, can we talk about this when I'm not half-asleep?'

'Yes, of course. Bye. I love you.'

I waited for him to say it back, but he didn't.

Later that night, when I looked out of my bedroom window, I thought I saw someone standing in the lane again. I opened the window and called, 'Leo? Is that you?' Whoever it was turned and walked away.

I crawled into bed, wishing I had Leo's arms to sink into. That night I had strange dreams of Miss Cartwright's false teeth riding away on a bicycle. Then Mrs Marrick and Miss Hooper appeared holding hands, with Mrs Marrick's son in tow, only I couldn't see his face clearly so it could have been someone else.

Meanwhile, I was aware of someone watching from the shadows outside the cottage, but I could not be sure if that was real or part of my dream. I woke up with the feeling that it was a bit of both.

11

I wasn't sure I should be going away for the weekend, with such a big case on, but the sarge told me to go. 'We could all use a break,' he said. 'Maybe it'll give us a chance to think up some new ideas.'

I have never met Annabel's parents, the Duke and Duchess of Midchester. All I knew of them was what she'd told me. They were disappointed that she had decided to become a doctor rather than marry some other duke's son, and every time she went home they reminded her of their disappointment in her lack of marital status and motherhood. She was an only child, so their estate would be entailed away to a distant cousin. Her parents had hoped she would marry this cousin and solve all their problems.

I spent most of the time leading up to the weekend fussing about what I was going to wear. The only truly formal wear I owned was my uniform. The rest of the time I lived in shirts and pedal-pushers. I had a couple of pretty going-out dresses, but I'd bought them from Woolworths. I felt sure that they would not do for a duke and duchess. Annabel came to the rescue, with a blue satin dress for Saturday night dinner.

'The rest of the time, wear your old clothes,' she said. 'I will be.'

I didn't point out that even when Annabel was wearing old clothes, she looked like a film star. She had glamour and poise, and at least five more inches of height than me.

We travelled to Shropshire in Annabel's Triumph. Her parents' extensive Georgian manor house was near to the town of Midchester, which was even smaller than Stony End.

I don't know why I had expected the duke to look like something out of *The Scarlet Pimpernel*. When he came out of the house, he was dressed in threadbare old tweeds. He looked a bit like Winston Churchill, only slimmer. The duchess was not much better dressed, though she did have a twinset and pearls to go with her old tweed skirt. Her greying hair was piled on her head in a messy style that still managed to make her look of noble blood. It made me feel immediately less self-conscious about my checked shirt and blue jeans, and my hair which I'd tied up in a ponytail.

'Annabel, darling,' she said, kissing her daughter on both cheeks. 'And this is Roberta?' She held out her hand to me. I think I would have curtseyed, but Annabel's firm hand on my elbow prevented me from dipping too low.

'Everyone calls me Bobbie,' I said.

'It's a pleasure to meet you, Roberta.'

That told me! I was to be Roberta for the rest of the weekend.

'Come on in,' said the duke. 'We'll show you around.'

The next half-hour was taken up with a tour of the house. Everything in it was just a bit worn, but in that genteel way that only the rich can get away with. I could tell that the house needed a lot of money spending on it to bring it back to its former glory.

We were taken to a drawing room full of old squashy sofas, where tea and cakes were laid out on a coffee table. The fire was lit, and two big dogs — lurchers, I think — were lying down in front of it. They looked up at me and seemed to decide I wasn't much worth bothering about, so they went back to sleep. I missed Elvis and his warm, wet nose.

When I sat down, I almost disappeared into the back of the sofa. I ended up perched on the end, so that it didn't swallow me up completely. No wonder rich people have such good posture, I thought.

'Annabel tells us you're a policewoman,' said the duke.

'Yes, Your Grace . . . I mean Sir . . . that's right.' I had a cup and saucer in one hand and a small plate with a slice of fruit cake in the other, and didn't really know what to do with either of them. The cup rattled in the saucer and the cake looked as if it was going to make a run for it. Normally cake soothed me, but it seemed that the ability not to lose this slice down the back of the sofa was all that stood between me and being socially ostracised. I felt sure the whole thing was being done to test my worth.

'Just call him 'Duke',' Annabel muttered.

'What will you do when you marry?' asked the duchess. She was looking at Annabel, which made me wonder if the question was really for her daughter.

'I haven't thought about it. No one has proposed to me yet.'

'You're going out with a doctor, aren't you?' asked the duke.

'Yes . . . Duke. Leo Stanhope. He's a wonderful doctor. And so is Annabel,' I added for good measure.

'Hmm,' the duke and duchess said in unison.

'A girl really needs to think about

marriage and children when she reaches a certain age, don't you think?' said the duchess. 'Annabel is twenty-eight now. Time is running out. How old are you, Roberta?'

My cup started to rattle even more, so I didn't get chance to answer as I tried to catch it before it hit the ground. Annabel deftly took it off me and put it on the coffee table. I put the cake in my lap, but dared not eat any in case I ended up talking with my mouth full.

'Annabel has had lots of offers,' said the duke. He either hadn't noticed my clumsiness or was too well-bred to draw attention to it. 'From men I mean. Johnny Frobisher's son would marry her in a heartbeat. He will inherit this dukedom one day.'

'I'm sure Roberta thinks she's doing well to ensnare a doctor,' said the duchess.

I almost meowed for her. 'I haven't ensnared Leo,' I said. 'We're not engaged or anything.'

'Hmm,' they both said again, each drinking their tea and taking a bite from a slice of cake. I wondered how they could do it so calmly and without actually appearing to eat or drink anything.

'Oh my God!' I said to Annabel, when she had finally taken me upstairs. We were in another threadbare but timelessly elegant room, with wood panelling and a huge four-poster bed that looked fit for a princess. 'How do you cope?'

'Now you know what I have to put up with,' she said, sitting on my bed. 'I'm so sorry they made you feel uncomfortable, sweetie.'

'Oh, don't worry about me.' My tummy rumbled, and I wished I had eaten the cake. 'I don't have to please them.' Despite that, I could feel the weight of their disapproval, and something in me wanted to make them proud, even though I was not their daughter. 'You poor thing.'

'I'll be glad when Tom and Leo get here.'

'I never did ask you how you and Tom managed to become friends,' I said.

'Oh . . . ' Annabel ran her fingers

through her hair. If I did not know her better, I would say she was acting coy. 'We met in Stony End when he returned from Sheffield that day. He apologised to me for his behaviour at the hospital, so I invited him in for a drink. He's all right, your brother. Drop dead dreamy, in fact.'

'Do you think so, Annabel?' I knew on some vague level that my brother was attractive to women, but as his sister I could not really see why.

'I wouldn't say it if I didn't mean it, sweetie. He's a very handsome man.'

'No, I mean, do you think he's all right in himself? He was really tense when he arrived in Stony End, and . . . well, Clyde Smith had a black eye, and . . . '

'You think Tom did it?' Annabel's lovely face fell. 'Oh, Bobbie, surely not.'

I told her all the things that had been worrying me. 'Tom's so determined to crack this case, and Carl said he's under a lot of pressure.'

'I'm sure he's fine, sweetie. Just eager to prove himself. By the way, did I tell you that Daddy has invited Leo and Tom to come shooting in the morning?'

'No, nothing's been said. I don't even know if Leo is coming to dinner.'

Annabel patted the bed, gesturing for me to sit next to her. 'What's happening with you two, Bobbie? I thought you were happy.'

'So did I, but things are a bit strained at the moment. He belittled my job to Joe, and then he thought I was up to something with Carl. There's always something that spoils the mood whenever we're together. We just can't seem to get on the same page lately. Every time I think we are, I find I've missed a few chapters. It's like reading a mystery with the final pages missing and . . . Oh dear, I think I've carried that metaphor quite far enough, don't you?'

Annabel smiled. 'At least you didn't mix it this time. Maybe things will work themselves out tomorrow. Stony End can be rather stifling at times.'

'I just hope your mother doesn't ask Leo if he's thinking of marrying me!'

'Oh, but that's a given, sweetie. It's Mummy's belief that everyone should be married to everyone else. Otherwise the world will end, or something.'

'Well, I suppose it would.'

That night, as we were sitting down to dinner in the oak-panelled dining room and I was debating what knives and forks to use, there was a knock on the door. The butler showed a young man into the room.

'Jack, how good to see you,' said the duke, standing up. 'Annabel, you remember Jack Frobisher, don't you? Johnny's boy.'

I had expected some sort of chinless wonder, but Jack Frobisher was a sight to behold, with long, windswept hair and a savagely handsome face; every bit the Byronic hero. When he smiled, he showed straight white teeth. 'Good to see you again, Annabel.'

'And you,' Annabel said tightly.

'Sorry to just drop in . . . '

'Nonsense, nonsense,' said the duke. 'You're just in time to join us for dinner.'

It was only then that I noticed another place had already been set. Annabel glowered, but her parents looked very happy.

'What have you been up to, Jack?' asked the duchess after the formal introductions had been made.

'Oh, this and that. Just had some shares come up trumps. That'll help keep the old pile going for a bit longer.'

'Jack's family have a palace in Berkshire,' the duchess informed me. 'Wonderful place — built by Vanbrugh, wasn't it, Jack?'

'Yes, with gardens by Brown. Capability Brown,' he said to me. He did not quite look down his nose at me, but I still got the sense that he thought I was beneath him.

'Yes, I've heard of him,' I said. 'Didn't Vanbrugh build Castle Howard and Blenheim Palace too?'

'Yes indeed.' I wasn't sure if the duke was impressed or surprised by my knowledge. 'Whereabouts are you from?'

'Derbyshire.'

'Oh yes, I know it well. Do you dine

with the Cavendishes at Chatsworth?'

'Not lately,' I admitted.

'Roberta is a police officer,' the duke explained to Jack, looking down at his food as if he had found a slug in his lettuce. I guessed that I was the slug in question.

'What? A girl police officer? How fascinating. And what about you, Annabel? Still training to be a nurse?'

'Doctor,' Annabel said sharply. I was used to my friend being ebullient and fearless, but in her parents' home she seemed fretful and unhappy. 'I've completed my training.'

'Well done you. Though I hate blood myself. I bet you see a lot of that in your line,' Jack said to me. 'Lots of murder and mayhem. Not a nice subject for a pretty girl like you.'

'Sometimes,' I said. 'At the moment I'm working on the Rat Pack robberies.' It was the name that the papers had given to the crimes. As the weeks went on and the criminals evaded arrest, tales of their escapades enthralled the public more and more, giving it all a rather fairytale quality. I knew I was only saying it to impress him, and I hated myself for it.

He leaned forward and rested his hand on his chin. 'Really? It's all rather exciting, isn't it? A group of crooks who make a smash-and-grab on a bank without hurting anyone? We'd all do it if we could get away with it.'

'Actually, they did hurt someone,' I said. 'The assistant manager.'

'Oh yes, I'd forgotten about that,' said Jack. 'That was in somewhere called Baggins End, wasn't it? He's not seriously hurt, though, is he?'

'It was Stony End, and he was injured quite considerably,' Annabel snapped. 'Really Jack, you could show some humanity.'

'Oh it'll be something for him to tell his grandchildren about.' Jack laughed as if he had made a joke.

'He doesn't have a wife and children,' I said.

'Well, you must tell us all about it,

Roberta,' said the duke. 'We don't get much excitement around here.'

'There's not much to tell,' I said, wishing I had never brought up the subject. 'A group of four thugs stormed into a bank, stole other people's hard-earned money, and injured a harmless elderly gentleman.'

'Touché,' said Jack, grinning. 'I think we've hit a raw nerve here, Duke.'

'Yes, it seems so. Now, perhaps you could tell me about these shares,' said the duke to Jack. 'I could do with a bit of advice. This old place is crumbling, and we need to get the roof repaired before winter comes back. Of course, if Annabel — '

'If Annabel what?' she snapped. 'Prostituted myself into a marriage?'

'Really, Annabel,' said the duchess. 'That's hardly the case.'

'Isn't it, Mother?'

'Your father and I had an arranged marriage, and we get along together really well, don't we, dear?'

'Let's not get into that,' said the

duke, as if he feared that Annabel might disagree with that assessment of her parents' marriage. Judging by the watery gleam in her eyes, he was probably right.

'I'll tell you about the shares when the ladies withdraw after dinner,' Jack promised. 'I'm sure they'd find all the financial talk deadly dull.'

The rest of dinner was uneventful. Jack kept trying to flirt with Annabel, who resolutely refused to be drawn in. The duke and duchess then went on to discuss people whom I did not know and would probably never meet, leaving me out of the conversation completely.

I must admit I was amused once I realised that 'Binky', 'Pogo', and 'Lulu' were the nicknames of some rather prominent members of the government. There were also some mutterings about Profumo and some girl called Christine Keeler. That scandal, at least for the rest of the public, was some way off, but it appeared to be an open secret amongst the upper classes. To me, on that night, they were just names of people I would never know, and therefore meant nothing.

I was only relieved that I managed to get through dinner without disgracing myself too much, taking Annabel's lead in what wine glasses to drink from and which cutlery to use in which course. Though I noticed that the duke and duchess did not care so much, and if they used the wrong fork or spoon it was discreetly replaced by the waiting staff.

'I can't believe they've done this,' Annabel fumed later that night when she came to wish me goodnight.

'Inviting Jack Frobisher?'

'Exactly. It was so bloody obvious why he turned up. They're trying to hook us up.'

'He's very handsome,' I ventured.

'Do you like him?' she asked.

I thought about it for a minute. 'No. No, I don't. It isn't that he's got a rose-coloured view of the bank robbery. A lot of people have — even me sometimes. It's something else that's not quite right. Call it a copper's instinct.'

'Then I'm glad I've got you to help me sort these things out, sweetie.' Annabel sighed. 'I hate being in this house, with Mummy and Daddy pretending they're the best of friends. They're really not, you know. They sleep in separate wings and usually only come together in the evening for dinner.' She sighed again. 'We'd best get some sleep. We're shooting in the morning.'

'Do we have to shoot animals?' I asked. 'I'd rather not.'

'Not if you don't want to. We can try some clay pigeon shooting.'

'That sounds better.'

Annabel left me and then I realised that I had forgotten my shawl, which I had put over the back of my chair in the drawing room. The mansion was such a maze of rooms and corridors that I first lost my way to the top of the stairs. By the time I found them I was getting tired of walking. Then when I got to the bottom of the stairs I forgot my way to the drawing room. I remembered we had to go through two doors from the dining room to get to it, one of green baize and the other of old oak, but when I looked there were several green baize doors. I chose the first one, and found a door that was slightly ajar, but I could see through the narrow gap that it led to a study. Someone was in there, talking to someone else. They had their backs to me and the room was dimly lit, so I could not see who they were.

Afraid of being seen, even though I was not doing anything illegal, I turned to leave when I heard whoever was in the room say, 'I don't know what's happening. The old man is keeping quiet about it.' There was a pause, and I realised that the speaker was talking to someone on the telephone. 'What? Oh yes, he's very interested in the shares . . . Hang on, I think someone's here.'

I rushed out of the green baize door and decided to get back to my room before I met anyone else. That took some doing, as I managed to lose my way again. I was exhausted by the time I finally found my bedroom.

I was relieved to see Leo arrive with Tom the next morning. They seemed to be getting on famously, having shared a long trip together from Stony End. I rushed over to Leo and kissed him full on the lips. Annabel and Tom said hello to each other, and she kissed him on the cheek a bit too effusively. I sensed she was doing it for Jack Frobisher's benefit, and for a moment I was peeved with her. I didn't want her leading my brother on just to make a point to another man. But then I saw the way she looked at Tom, and I could see that there was genuine admiration there.

'I'm glad you're here,' I said to Leo.

'Yes, me too.' He seemed to search my face. 'How's life with the upper classes?'

'Not too bad. I've managed not to disgrace myself too much.'

'You never would, Bobbie,' Leo said. 'You always know how to behave in any situation.'

I kissed him again. 'I could have done with you saying those things yesterday when I was a bag of nerves.'

The introductions with the duke and duchess and Jack Frobisher were made, and then the shooting party began. It turned out that Annabel and I weren't expected to shoot anything. The women of the shooting party were only expected to help the men load their weapons. There were a few neighbours in attendance, to make up the numbers.

I was struck by just how comfortable everyone seemed in the situation. Leo behaved as if he was born to it, but he had been brought up with upper-middle-class parents. Tom fitted in because his shooting was up to competition standard. And of course Annabel, her parents, and Jack Frobisher had been born to it. Annabel insisted on partnering Tom, which earned a scowl from Frobisher. He managed to snag himself a pretty girl from one of the neighbouring families, so he was not too heartbroken.

Only I felt like a spare wheel, standing aside and helping where I could but generally feeling as if I was in the way. When I messed up trying to load Leo's gun for the third or fourth time, a neighbour stepped in, leaving me completely at a loose end. I sat on a stone wall, watching them all and wondering why I was even there. I didn't like the noise, and it was impossible to have a conversation, because everyone was so absorbed in their shooting. I was afraid it would be bad manners to go back to the house.

Would life as Leo's wife be like this? I wondered. He was from a different class to me, yet somehow managed to move between circles with ease and comfort; something his training as a doctor had allowed. Despite what he said about me always knowing how to behave, I was not so sure. I felt gauche and lumpy amongst the elegant women who attended the shoot. Even in their old tweeds, they had more bearing than I did.

The shooters had moved down into a meadow, where beaters were scaring up some birds. I decided to go for a walk, so I followed the lane around. It was one of those typical British days where a harsh wind blew across the fields, but the sun shone down, hot on one's head.

The sound of guns filled the air, making it hard for me to think clearly. I could hear even less, though I suddenly became aware of my name being called from somewhere. I looked around just as a bullet whizzed past and chipped my earlobe. I think it was the shock more than anything that made me fall down to the ground. Apparently there are tiny capillaries in the earlobes, which can result in startling blood loss, so when I pulled my hand away it was bright red. I think I might have fainted. I know the world around me started to spin.

I came to with everyone standing over me, and Leo knelt at my side, checking my pulse.

'Silly girl,' I heard someone say. 'She

should have known better.'

'Well, that's what happens when you let the riffraff in,' someone else said.

Telling myself it didn't matter what strangers thought, I looked to Leo, Tom, and Annabel for reassurance.

'Oh Bobbie, what a silly thing to do.' Annabel folded her arms, looking disappointed in me.

'Nice one, sis,' said Tom, raising a sardonic eyebrow.

Leo's eyes were dark pits of fury. 'Of all the stupid things to do,' he said.

★　★　★

I only managed to get through the rest of the day by telling myself it would soon be over. I must admit I got rather dramatic about it all, lying on the bed like some Regency heroine sent there with a 'megrim'. It was one way of avoiding everyone. Leo stayed with me a while, pressing down on my earlobe until it stopped bleeding, but I was in no mood to speak to him, so he went downstairs with the others.

Instead I fell into a major bout of self-pity, and if I could go back to that time, I'd give myself a good shake. But there are times when we all feel the whole world is against us and even one wrong word will back up that theory. I'd had several wrong words directed at me, by people who were supposed to care about me. Even if they were justified in that I had been stupid to wander around a place where people were shooting guns in all directions, at the time I felt they were being unjust, because I was the one who had been injured. Yet I had not received one word of sympathy — only constant reminders of my stupidity.

I decided that I would find somewhere else to live so I did not have to face Annabel anymore. Tom was my brother and always would be, but he would soon go back to London, so I wouldn't have to worry about him. As for Leo, it was clear to me that things were over. I could hardly bear to look at him. I knew that if I did, the tears would fall, and I was more than ever determined that this big girl would not cry. It was embarrassing enough to have fainted. Some big, tough policewoman I was!

Of course I became the joke of the day. When I went downstairs for afternoon tea, I tried to meet everyone's quips with rejoinders of my own, but it's fair to say I was not at the top of my game.

We were just about to go into dinner when Leo received a call. 'I apologise,' he said to our hosts, 'but I'm needed at Stony End hospital.'

'Am I needed?' asked Annabel hopefully. 'I'm sure I must be.'

'It's OK, Annabel,' said Leo with a small grin. He seemed to guess she was trying to escape. 'You stay here with your family. Will you be all right?' It was a moment before I realised that Leo was speaking to me. 'Bobbie, will you be all right?'

'Why wouldn't I be?'

'Well, you were shot today.' That led to more laughter and jokes.

'I'm fine. Annabel is a doctor, too, so I'm sure if I have a relapse, she can help me.'

'A relapse? Are you planning on getting shot again?' asked Jack Frobisher.

'Who knows what the evening may bring?' I asked. 'I may not survive the fish course.'

'Yes, they can be tricky, those rainbow trout,' said Leo. He was smiling at me, but I didn't return it. When he went to kiss me goodbye, I turned my head, so the kiss landed on my one good ear. I could see his confusion as he pulled away, but I couldn't understand it. I felt sure he must have known he had hurt me when he called me stupid. 'I'll see you when you get back to Stony End tomorrow.'

'Perhaps,' I said in a low voice. I could see he wanted to say more, but we had an audience and he was in a hurry. After once again making his apologies to the duke and duchess, he left us.

Dinner was a little bit less fraught without him there. With more people attending, it did not stand out so much that I sat mainly in silence, only speaking when I was spoken to.

We were on the fish course — I picked at my trout gingerly — when the butler told us that another visitor had arrived. 'Detective Carl Latimer,' he announced.

'He probably wants me,' said Tom, getting up from the table.

'Let the poor man eat some dinner,' said Jack Frobisher. 'Then talk business.' It was almost as if he owned the duke's home already. No one contradicted him.

Carl was brought in and another place set for him. He smiled at me shyly. 'I heard you had a dreadful accident,' he said.

'Not dreadful,' I said. 'Just silly.'

'It's hardly silly to be shot, Bobbie. People should be more careful with firearms.'

I remember breathing a sigh of relief that someone was on my side. 'Thanks, Carl,' I said.

After dinner, my sore ear gave me an

excuse to go to bed early, so I said my goodbyes and left the others to their port and coffee.

Carl walked me to the foot of the stairs. 'Are you all right, Bobbie? Really?'

'I will be,' I said. I put my hand on his arm. 'Thank you for your kind words, Carl. They're the first I've heard all day.'

To my surprise, he kissed me on the cheek. There was something intimate about the kiss that made me inadvertently recoil. I had the sudden image of someone standing outside the cottage, but pushed it away. It couldn't be Carl. He was a decent man. Wasn't he?

'Sorry,' he said. 'Sorry. I overstepped the mark.'

'No, no, of course not. I just . . . it's been a tense day. Goodnight, Carl.'

I was just dozing off when Annabel flung open my bedroom door. I was half-expecting a telling-off for being such an embarrassment. I steeled myself against the onslaught, so it threw me completely when I saw that Tom was standing next to her.

'What is it?'

'Carl came with bad news,' said Annabel. 'Poor old Mr Preston is dead.'

'So the bank robbery is now a murder enquiry,' said Tom.

12

'I should have spoken to him when I had the chance,' said Tom as the three of us travelled back to Stony End in Annabel's car the following morning. Carl had already left. 'And I should have let Carl tell me sooner last night.'

'I suppose that's my fault,' said Annabel. 'And my family's.'

'No,' said Tom, reaching over and touching her hand. They were in the front seat of the car, whilst I sat in the back. 'I'm not saying that, love.' Love? I really had missed a chapter or two! 'You were protecting your patient, which is what you're supposed to do,' he continued. 'But we might have missed something important by not going back to him sooner. As for your family, well, I suppose it was bad form to interrupt their dinner. It's odd that Carl didn't insist on telling me sooner.'

I thought I knew why, but I still refused to completely believe it. And whatever problems my brother had when he arrived in Stony End, he certainly seemed to be behaving himself for Annabel's sake. Maybe she was what he needed to keep him on the straight and narrow.

'He'll have had visitors,' I said. 'Maybe he said something to them. We should speak to Mr Otterburn.'

'I wonder if he said anything to his visitors,' Tom said. 'His cousin might know something.'

'I just said that!'

'What? Oh, sorry, Bobbie. I wasn't listening.'

'How's the ear this morning?' Annabel asked brightly.

'It's OK, thanks.'

'Fancy walking into the path of a bullet, you daft old thing.'

'Yes, I've been apprised of my stupidity several times now.'

'Bobbie, I don't mean . . . We're just glad you're all right, aren't we, Tom?'

'Quite right. Can't have our Bobbie out of the game.'

I know I should have taken their banter as a sign that I was forgiven for my clumsiness, but I was in no mood to be placated. My ear hurt like hell, and my pride was even more bruised. I wrapped my coat around me, even though it wasn't that cold, and curled up in the corner of the back seat, pretending to go to sleep whilst they chattered happily together for the rest of the trip.

It was only then that I truly realised they were falling in love. It made me feel melancholy, because apart from their first irate meeting, there seemed to be no tension or strain to their falling in love. It was happening so easily. Even Annabel's parents hadn't managed to drive a wedge between them, despite their best efforts to keep pushing Jack Frobisher forward. But even I could see that Frobisher was no match for Tom. Frobisher might have the breeding, but Tom had something else. He had experience, and a confidence that came from a man who was at the top of his profession.

Frobisher's arrogance was born of his belief in his birthright, which is not quite the same thing as being confident in oneself. In the early 1960s, society was changing, and the upper classes were no longer given the deference they had once enjoyed. Mervin Griffiths-Jones's comment during the *Lady Chatterley's Lover* trial about whether it was a book that one would want their wives or servants to read had shown how far out of touch the upper classes were with those over whom they ruled. Women made their own choices about what they read, and servants were in charge of their own lives. They no longer had to kowtow to those 'upstairs', outside of their normal duties.

Frobisher and Annabel's parents still lived in a time when marriages of convenience were made and a woman's right to her own career was not even considered. Men like Frobisher would have to evolve and prove themselves useful in the world, or else they would become extinct. I might have felt sorry for Frobisher if he had not been such a git about Mr Preston's injuries.

To be fair, he had behaved with due respect when the subject of Mr Preston's death was mentioned at the breakfast table before we left. 'I'm very sorry to hear it,' he said. 'One doesn't expect such things to happen.'

'The bank robbery is not so exciting now,' I muttered.

'Oh, I don't know about that,' he'd said. 'It's just unfortunate things turned bad for the old man.'

When we arrived back in Stony End, I went upstairs to put on my uniform, whilst Tom went ahead to the station. I was still of the mind that I might find somewhere else to live after I'd managed to ruin the weekend at Annabel's parents' home.

She knocked on my door and came into my bedroom. 'Are you sure you're well enough to go out, sweetie?' she asked.

'Yes, I'm fine. It'll do me good to get back to work.' I buttoned up my tunic and put on my cap. I already felt better, apart from the fact that the rim of my cap felt heavy on my sore ear.

'Well, you just be careful.'

'Don't worry, Annabel. I'm not planning on getting shot again.'

'Bobbie . . . what's wrong?'

'What's wrong? Well, I was shot yesterday. That sort of put the dampers on the weekend. And then I had to listen to the three people I love most letting me know how stupid I was. Silly me, getting shot. Like I'd planned to do it! I was on a public footpath, Annabel, not on the range where you all were. I was on a path, and a stray bullet hit me. Yet somehow that's not the fault of the shooter, who didn't keep their gun pointed at the birds or the clay pigeons or whatever. It's my fault for being stupid!'

'Oh darling girl, we were only reacting like that because you frightened us when you fell, that's all. We thought the worst.'

'What, and your relief made you all insult me?'

'No, no. When I said it was silly I didn't mean it like that.'

'Well then, how *did* you mean it, Annabel? Because I've tried to work out how it could mean anything other than that you think I'm an imbecile, but I've got nowhere.'

'Oh now you are being stupid, Bobbie! I never said you were an imbecile. None of us did. Don't be so overdramatic!'

'Yes, that's me to a tee.' She was right, but I would never admit it. 'Strange how being shot does that to a person.' I stormed from the room and flew down the stairs, my body tingling with anger.

I'd cooled down a little by the time I got to the station, but it seemed I had not quite finished for the day. Tom was there, with Carl and some of the other coppers. 'I thought you'd gone home to rest,' he said. 'We're just going to speak to Mr Otterburn and some of the other witnesses again. Just in case we missed something.'

'OK, who do you want me to speak to?'

'No one, Bobbie. You shouldn't even be here. You should be at home resting.'

'I'm part of this investigation, Tom.'

'No, it's fine.'

'Yes,' said one of the men, 'you go home and rest your ear, Blandford. These battlefield wounds take some mending.' That was followed by laughter.

'I'm quite capable of working,' I said. My knees were shaking as I struggled to control my fury.

'Of course you are,' said Tom in placatory tones. 'But we've got it covered.'

'Besides,' said another copper, 'they're poaching up near Little Stony today. You don't want to get shot again.' More laughter. It seemed I was to be the butt of everyone's jokes for quite some time.

'How long did it take you to tell everyone, Tom?' I snapped. 'Five minutes? Five seconds?'

'Don't be silly, Bobbie,' Tom said. 'You're showing yourself up.'

'Hey,' said Carl, 'come on, Tom. The lady could have been killed. It's not really a laughing matter. For any of you,' he added more firmly, looking around at my colleagues. 'It seems to me that someone needs to be more careful where they point a gun. I'm glad you're OK, Bobbie.'

'Thanks,' I whispered. I could feel the tears stinging the back of my eyes, but I would not cry in front of my colleagues. They all traipsed out of the station, leaving me to my misery. It occurred to me that I only needed to row with Leo and it would be a hat trick.

I didn't want to go home and I didn't want to stay at the station. I was not in the mood for Mrs Higgins and her flights of fancy, either. My own imagination was running overtime, as I silently planned to pack all my things and run away from not just Annabel's cottage, but Stony End. First I would find everyone who had upset me and tell them exactly what I thought of them. I went through whole conversations, though in my imagination it was mostly me talking whilst they could only listen, probably with tears in their eyes as they realised I was right all along about how mean they had been to me. But it was too late, I'd tell them. I was leaving. Forever. They would beg me to stay, of course, but I'd be resolute and get on the train, looking dreamily into the distance as I travelled towards a new life with people who cared about me getting shot in the ear.

My feet took me not to the train station but to the prefab estate. Alf and Greta Norris were in the garden when I got there. He was digging out a flower-bed, and she was trimming the privet hedge. 'Oh, Bobbie,' said Greta, dropping her shears and rushing to throw her arms around me. 'Someone said you'd been shot. Thank God you're all right.'

'My pride is more bruised than my ear,' I said, nestling into her welcoming arms.

'Come on inside. Alf, put the kettle on. I've got some nice fruitcake.'

Accompanied by nurturing phrases from Greta, I was led into the house and given the most comfortable chair, along with tea and cake, as I told them what had happened at the shooting party.

'I'm sure the duke and duchess were beside themselves,' said Greta as soon as I was comfortable.

'Not really,' I said. 'In fact, you'd think I'd committed a faux pas of the grandest order, being shot on their land.' It was only then that it occurred to me how unconcerned Annabel's parents had been. If someone came into my home and was hurt, I would be mortified and want to do everything I could to make them feel better. Yet after I'd been shot, the duke and duchess had treated me with coldness, as if I were responsible for ruining the day for everyone. The more I thought about it, the more they seemed to have lacked not just good manners, but common human decency. 'That's what you get for being a nobody.'

'You are not a nobody,' said Greta. Her response explained why I had walked to their house rather than the station.

'I'm sure Leo was upset,' said Alf.

'Furious, more like.'

'With the shooter?' said Greta. 'As he should be.'

I sighed. 'No, with me.' That was when I poured out the rest of my woes. Alf and Greta were always easy to talk to; like an aunt and uncle who looked out for me in the absence of my mother. She lived in Chesterfield, and I did not always want to bother her with my problems. Mum had not wanted me to join the police force, and although we had come to an understanding about it, I still felt uncomfortable talking to her about my work. If she knew I'd been shot, even though it was not in the line of duty, it would only prove to her that I should be in a nice, safe job. 'Then I had to put up with ribbing from everyone at the dinner last night and at the station today.'

'Well, you know what they're like at the station, Bobbie,' said Alf. 'It's not just you, duck. They're like that to everyone. You weren't there when Ernie Turner's wife left him for a French bloke. She came back, but she had a baby girl soon after. Ernie almost transferred to another station, because every time he walked in the blokes started singing 'Thank Heaven for Little Girls' in a French accent.'

'Oh God.' I covered my face to hide my own smile. Alf cheered me up with a few more stories of teasing at the station. The fact that I couldn't help laughing made me put things into perspective. It was funny when you weren't the one on the receiving end.

'Anyway, pet,' said Alf, 'it's our anniversary in a couple of months. We're having a big do at the village hall. You're coming, aren't you?'

'Of course I am,' I said. Alf and Greta had met during the war. Greta, who had been born in Austria, was considered a threat to national security simply because of her birthplace. It had been Alf's job to check up on her every day. They had fallen in love, and it had nearly cost Alf his career with the police, until he came to Stony End.

I had once been told that Stony End was the place you came to when nowhere else would have you. I had moved there after a failed love affair with a married Italian had ruined my career as a hotel receptionist. I had found friendship and love in Stony End and an acceptance of my place in a man's profession that was lacking in other towns. It occurred to me that I really would be stupid if I gave all that up over a few ill-chosen remarks.

I left Alf and Greta in much better shape than when I arrived, and made my way back to the station. I was not yet ready to go home and face Annabel. I did worry that she might throw me out after my outburst, but I tried not to think about it too much. In that scenario I saw myself sneaking onto the train in disgrace as I burned yet another bridge.

Instead I went downstairs into the cellar where all the old case files were, and started hunting for the details of the wartime bank robbery. I found a few files from about five years before, about Jimmy Ogden, that were interesting even though they had no bearing on the case at hand. He had been a very naughty boy in the past and on at least one occasion had been found with drugs, or dope as we called it in those days, on his person. The drug problem in the early '60s was not as bad as it became later in the era, when pop stars like the Beatles and the Rolling Stones made the drug lifestyle seem glamorous, but it was still a concern. It seemed from the files that Jimmy had only had enough drugs on him for personal use, which meant he was allowed to go without charge, but it was in a cold case file because the officer in charge at the time had been sure there were other dealers around and that Jimmy knew who they were. The case was kept open in the hopes he might give information one day.

There was something interesting in one of Jimmy's files. In 1959 he had been arrested for stealing clothes, which he said had fallen off the back of a lorry. He had been arrested at the same time as a William Ogden, aged forty-nine. Further reading told me that William was Jimmy's father.

Mrs Ogden had said her husband did not come back from the war. I had taken that to mean he was dead, but obviously he was not. Interesting as this was, though, it had nothing to do with the bank robbery that I could see. Jimmy's crimes were strictly small-time. So I put the file aside and began looking for the one about the wartime robbery.

I lost track of time, once again enthralled by the cases before me. At least it took my mind off my sore ear. By the time I found what I wanted, my neck was aching and my knees had seized up. I got up somewhat shakily and opened the file, reading through quickly to find the information I wanted.

It turned out that there had been no assistant manager at the bank during the war. Whoever it was had gone off to join the fighting, I supposed. But his place had been taken by a chief clerk; a woman. It was she who was injured during the robbery. Some sort of synchronicity seemed to be at play, because on the day of the latest bank robbery in Stony End, Alf and I had been checking out a house-break in Little Stony involving the same woman. I had been told she had worked in a bank, but it had not registered at the time that it was in Stony End.

The bank clerk who had been injured during the robbery in the war was none other than Mrs Marrick.

13

'Mrs Marrick clearly did not take part in the recent bank robbery,' said the sarge the next morning when I showed him the file. 'She has a good alibi.'

'Yes, because me and Alf were there,' I agreed. 'But it's odd, isn't it, that it happened at the same time. She said that her son, Alan Marrick, had got in, and left without telling them, leaving the door open. But I'm sure they said that the door had been forced open. The trouble is, when we got the call about the bank robbery, we left very quickly, and hadn't had time for a proper look. We were remiss in our duties.'

'We're stretched thin, Blandford, so don't blame yourself. As you said, nothing was taken from Mrs Marrick's house; so whilst someone broke in, or appeared to, there wasn't a theft.'

'I wondered if I could go up and talk to her, Sarge. Find out what happened in the war. Unless you think I should involve Scotland Yard.' I prayed that he would say no.

'No, I wouldn't involve them at this point, Blandford.' The sarge's eyes twinkled as if he knew what I had been thinking. 'That was eighteen years ago, and we've no idea if it was even the same gang. Let's not bother our Scotland Yard friends over a hunch.'

'I'll go now,' I said, feeling very pleased with myself. I would crack this case wide open and show Annabel, Tom, and Leo that I was not stupid at all.

'How's the ear?'

'Hurts like he . . . heck,' I said.

'You can say 'hell' in front of me, Blandford. I'm unshockable. Get it checked out by the duty surgeon before you go.'

'There's no need, Sarge. I'm fine.' I wondered if the sarge knew that Leo was the duty surgeon that day. He had telephoned the night before, but I had not seen him since he'd left Annabel's parents'.

'There was a pile-up on the Stockport road involving a pregnant woman,' Leo had explained. 'I'm sorry I couldn't get to see you.'

'I've been busy anyway,' I said. I almost told him about Mrs Marrick and my breakthrough, but I was in no mood to share with him.

'You should be resting.'

'I'm fine.'

We had somehow got to the end of a very strained conversation and said goodnight.

I was about to slip out of the station and ignore the sarge's orders when Leo came from the cells and called me. 'Bobbie, the sarge wants me to check your ear.'

'It's fine. I'm fine.'

'So you keep saying, but you don't sound it.'

'I'm very busy with important things to do. I have suspects to interrogate and a lead on the bank robbery to follow.' I hated the sound of my own self-importance, but I wanted to show him that I was not stupid.

'Really? What leads?'

'I can't say yet.' I didn't admit that it might lead nowhere.

'Let me change that dressing at least,' he said. 'It looks as though your ear's been bleeding again.'

I put my finger to it and realised he was right. Reluctantly, I followed him into the kitchenette, which was the only place in the station where we could sit and rest. He attended to my dressing, then kissed me on the forehead, but neither of us spoke much.

'Here,' he said when he had finished. He took a lollipop out of his pocket. He often carried them for when he had to deal with children. 'This is for being a good girl.'

'I'm not a child, Leo.'

'Sorry, I thought I was being charming. Or at least, I'm trying very hard to be, so I can be forgiven for whatever it is I've done this time.'

'You called me stupid. Remember? I mean, you're right,' I said, standing up, but only finding myself closer to him. 'People who go around getting themselves shot are really stupid.'

'Bobbie, I didn't mean — '

'You didn't mean it the way it sounded. That's exactly what Annabel said. Maybe the two of you should look up the words 'silly' and 'stupid' in a dictionary.'

'When I saw you fall to the ground, I feared the worst. My reaction was just born of relief, Bobbie. I didn't mean it to come out quite like that. In fact, I can hardly remember what I said now.'

'Yes, well, maybe you should start practising your bedside manner a bit more. It left a lot to be desired yesterday. I have to go now.' I was about to leave, but my temper was up, so I spun around. 'When you were injured the other year, I was beside myself, yet never once did it occur to me to call you stupid for what happened. Even when you took off to America for months, leaving me to worry about you. I didn't even tell you that you were stupid for marrying a woman you'd only known for twenty-four hours, even though that was particularly stupid of you. But I get accidentally shot, and — '

'Bobbie — '

'No, you listen to me. You've told me that my job isn't good enough for your brother, and now you've told me I'm stupid because of an accident that could have happened to anyone. Have you any idea what that does to my self-esteem? I really don't need to be with someone who makes me feel so low about myself. I can do better.'

Leo's eyes flashed angrily. 'What? Like Carl Latimer, you mean?'

'Carl? What?' I could not see where he was coming from, because I had honestly not considered Carl in a romantic light. He was just a nice bloke who I enjoyed working with. That I had my own misgivings about him was irrelevant. 'There is no Carl. Carl is nothing to me.'

Of course, the next thing I did was turn and see Carl standing in the kitchenette doorway. He looked as if I'd kicked him in the gut.

'Sorry,' I said, pushing past him. 'Sorry, I didn't mean . . . '

It was a relief to get onto my Vespa and drive up to Little Stony. The fresh air cooled my cheeks, and the scenery always had a calming effect on my soul. Poor Carl. I had not meant to insult him in that way. When I had said he was nothing, I had meant he was nothing to me. In a way it helped me to see how a badly chosen word could be misconstrued. But I was still at a loss as to how 'stupid' could mean anything but that.

I was halfway to Little Stony when I realised that it was a market day, and that Mrs Marrick would probably be on the stall rather than at home. Nevertheless, I went to the house and knocked on the door, but there was no answer. I walked around the side of the house and noticed that there was an old van parked in one of the garages. The garage door had been left open. The van looked like it had once belonged to the Royal Mail, but had been painted over with very dark paint. I could not tell if it was blue or black. I had not noticed it on my last visit, so I presumed it must belong to Alan Marrick. I made a note to report it when I got back to the station.

There was no sign of the ladies, so I went back down to Stony End, where the market was in full swing. Stalls with brightly coloured canopies, selling cheeses, fresh meat, cakes, vegetables, and salad were spread across the town square. I waved to Mrs Higgins, who was on her own stall.

'I'm selling a nice fruit loaf today,' she said. 'Sales haven't been all that good, though.'

'Put one aside for me for later,' I said. 'I'll pick it up on the way home.' Realising from her disappointed expression that I had not yet bought enough, I said, 'I'll have some of your apricot jam too. And marmalade. We need marmalade.'

'I'll throw in the marmalade for free, since it's you.'

'Mrs Higgins, I'm trying to help you here.'

'I know you are, which is why you get free marmalade. You're a good girl, Bobbie Blandford.'

Mrs Marrick and Miss Hooper had a stall in the built-in market, on the upper floor. There were no stairs to worry about. One reached the upper floor by walking all the way around, as the floor sloped gently upwards, and the stalls stretched around in a spiral, albeit a rather square formation. The aromas of fish, raw meat, and freshly baked goods filled the air.

I passed some cages holding puppies and kittens, each one of them rushing forward and putting their paws on the bars, to see if I would be their new owner. This type of selling was allowed back then, so I never really considered that it might be the wrong way to treat animals. I did wish I could take them all, but my job did not allow for pets.

We could only take care of Elvis because he spent half his time at Dottie's.

I passed my favourite record stall, and waved to the proprietor. 'You OK, Barney?'

'Not bad, Bobbie. Just got back from Liverpool. A mate told me I had to go to the Cavern Club and listen to this band, the Beatles. Oh, they were brilliant. They're going to be huge, Bobbie. You heard it here first.'

'Oh yeah,' I said, grinning. 'The poor lads. What have they ever done to you? That's the kiss of death coming from you.' Barney always had some tips for upcoming pop stars, and they always sank without a trace. Then he'd be stuck with a load of albums or singles he needed to sell. I was usually the mug who bought them off him. I didn't mind. Sometimes the bands were really good, and it was only luck or bad timing that prevented them from making it big.

'Nah, I'm right this time. You mark my words. Liverpool bands are going to rule the world.'

Mrs Marrick and Miss Hooper were busy on their stall when I reached it, so I had to wait for the customers to finish their purchases. Miss Hooper sold the fruit and veg, whilst Mrs Marrick sold the cakes, jams and chutneys. Everything was set out in perfect rows, with neat little labels. The clientele came from the higher reaches of Stony End society, and the prices reflected that. I recognised the handwriting on the labels from the one found at the derelict house.

'Is there a problem?' Mrs Marrick asked when she saw me at the end of the queue.

'It can wait,' I said. It was difficult then to get rid of the customers, as they were all agog as to why the police should be speaking to a lady who was well-respected in the area. I managed to glare at them all long enough so they got the message. Mrs Marrick put a 'back in five minutes' sign on the stall and we went further up the walkway to the top of the market, where there was a café.

'I've been looking at other robberies in the area,' I said when we sat down with our cups of frothy coffee and Chelsea buns. The views from the café took in a good bit of the town and the Peaks behind it. 'And I came across a file about the bank robbery during the war. In 1944? Do you remember it?'

'Yes, I remember it,' said Mrs Marrick. 'I was there, of course. But I suppose you know that, or you would not have come to speak to me. Am I a suspect in the latest robbery?'

I smiled. 'You had a very good alibi, in me and Alf Norris.'

'That's a relief.' Mrs Marrick smiled, but she seemed to be under a lot of strain.

'You were injured during the previous robbery, weren't you?' I asked.

'Yes, I was. The brutes hit me over the head with a cosh.'

'Henri was in hospital for several days, weren't you, dear?' said Miss Hooper. 'It was a very worrying time.'

'Then I'm sorry to bring it up again,'

I said, even though that was not strictly true. 'Can you remember a lot about that day, Mrs Marrick? Anything you tell me would be of tremendous help.'

'It was a Friday.'

'Wages day?' I suggested.

'Yes, that is correct. The brewery payroll was in, waiting for the van to pick it up. I think it was about ten in the morning when it all took place. The men . . . I assume they were men . . . came into the bank and demanded we hand over money.'

'Did they speak to the manager?'

'He wasn't in. Something had called him away that day. I forget why he had to leave. I was in charge. Or as in charge as they let any woman be . . . Men didn't much like us taking on their roles during the war. Especially when they came back. I gave up the job because I was expected to go back to a junior position simply by dint of my gender.'

'Well . . .' Miss Hooper coughed politely. Mrs Marrick glanced at her sharply.

'Oh, nothing,' said Miss Hooper. 'I was a little confused, that's all.' What she was confused about I did not find out that day.

'So you were in charge, Mrs Marrick?'

'Yes, that is correct. They asked me for the combination to the safe, which I, of course, refused to give to them. Then they hit me with the cosh.'

'But they still got into the safe?'

'They threatened the other tellers, so I had no choice but to give them the combination. If I had my time again I would do things differently,' she said in a faraway voice.

'You were right not to argue. It's only money in the end. Poor Mr Preston has shown us that a life is much more important. What can you tell me about the robbers?'

'Very little. Four men, I believe. They all wore masks, so I didn't see their faces.'

'Rat Pack?' I suggested. 'No, it couldn't have been. Not then.'

'Bing Crosby, Bob Hope and Dorothy

Lamour. There were two Dorothys, if I remember correctly. It was rather silly, as they had all this plastic fruit attached to the masks.'

'Perhaps it wasn't Dorothy Lamour,' Miss Hooper suggested. 'Perhaps it was Carmen Miranda.'

'She didn't star in any films with Bing Crosby and Bob Hope, did she?' asked Mrs Marrick. 'No, dear, I'm sure it must have been Dorothy.'

'Was there anything familiar about their voices?' I asked, not really wanting to get into a discussion about who starred with whom. 'Could you tell their ages?'

Mrs Marrick paused, as if she was giving the matter great thought. She looked over my shoulder, whether seeking heavenly guidance I do not know. 'I honestly cannot recall, after eighteen years of trying to forget the incident, WPC Blandford. At the time I thought one voice was familiar, but I couldn't tell you who I thought it was. One's mind plays tricks on one after so many years, as I'm sure you understand.'

'Yes, of course.'

'What's all this?' said a voice behind me. 'What have you been up to, Mater?'

I turned to see Alan Marrick standing behind me, holding a cup of tea. 'Your mother is not in any trouble, sir,' I assured him.

Without asking if he could join us, he squeezed into the booth next to me, more or less blocking off my exit. I don't know why I saw it as aggressive, as he seemed friendly enough, but I had a sudden longing to get out of there. 'Oh, pity. I always wanted to be one of those disadvantaged children. There's a lot of sympathy in it, I hear.' He looked at his mother as he spoke, and there was something in his voice — an undercurrent — that I could not quite put my finger on.

'You don't need anything I do to make you feel sorry for yourself, Alan,' Mrs Marrick said.

It seemed that Mr Marrick was not exactly a welcome guest, even with his own mother. I reminded myself to call at the station and mention the van.

'Are you staying in Little Stony for long, Mr Marrick?' I asked.

'Depends.' He put his hands behind his head and stretched like a very satisfied cat. There were lynxes running wild in Derbyshire and I wondered if he was related to them in some way. 'It's very comfortable here, with old Hooper fussing around me, making sure I don't upset Mater too much.'

'I'm sure you were very upset when your mother was injured during the wartime bank robbery. Where were you then? In the services?' I guessed he would have been in his mid-twenties around then.

'Fighting for king and country?' He scoffed. 'Not me. I wasn't fit enough for the draft. Bad ear. Or foot. Or something.' He grinned at his mother, who was finding something very interesting in the pattern on her plate. 'Truth is that Mater knew someone on the draft board. She's always handy for that sort of thing.'

'I'm sure WPC Blandford is not interested,' said Mrs Marrick. 'Is that all?' she asked me.

'I think so,' I said. I had not really learned a lot from her, but I had not expected to. It was her son I found most interesting. He was very charming and handsome, but I sensed he was also very cruel. There was some subtext to everything he said to his mother that bordered on sadism. His admittance that he had not fought in the war also lowered him in my estimation. It might seem that in the twenty-first century we are more accepting of those who have no wish to fight politicians' wars for them. We understand better that not all wars are justified.

The attitudes of my time were different. Men were expected to have done their bit, and I say without apology that I was a child of my time. Though I had been very young during the war, it was within my living memory and within the living memories of all those I knew. Everyone had lost someone between 1939 and 1945. We understood first-hand the sacrifices that millions of men made, and the pain that their families suffered when they received the dreaded telegram. We had seen the pictures of Jews being liberated from the camps, proving once and for all that the Allies had been justified in fighting against such evil. So to hear someone bragging about how he had dodged the draft was shocking to me.

I stood up awkwardly and at first it seemed that Alan Merrick was not going to move. He grinned up at me, as if enjoying catching me in his trap. He finally relented and let me out. 'If you think of anything that might help, Mrs Marrick,' I said, 'please contact me at the station. We don't know that the robbery then is connected to the robbery now, but it might be.'

'Of course,' said Mrs Marrick, also standing up. 'Please forgive my son for his irreverence.'

'Forgive me?' Alan Marrick laughed. 'As if I'm the one who needs forgiveness in this family.'

'Perhaps we could tell WPC Blandford all our sins,' said Mrs Marrick. 'Just to make you feel better, Alan.' She glared at her son.

'I'm a policewoman, not a priest,' I quipped, wishing I was anywhere but listening to this family tragedy. It was like being in the middle of a Shakespeare play, but without the blank verse.

'A very pretty one at that,' said Alan Marrick. He held his hands up in a surrender motion. 'Sorry, Mater. I can see I've outlived my welcome here. It's time I moved on.'

'There is one more thing, Mrs Marrick,' I said. 'When we searched the robbers' hideout, we found an empty jar of the jam you sell on your stall.'

'Really?'

'I wondered, when your house was broken into, whether someone took it and you didn't notice.'

'We've already told you that it was a mistake,' said Mrs Marrick. 'It was Alan turning up unannounced.'

'Oh yes, sorry. I remember now. Well, if you have sold preserves to any strangers lately, perhaps you could let me know. It might help us to track them down.'

I made my goodbyes and started towards the exit. I looked back to Mrs Marrick and Miss Hooper sitting in the booth. Miss Hooper took hold of Mrs Marrick's hand. It was a simple, innocent gesture of friendship, yet there was something else about it that I could not quite fathom. Alan Marrick was watching me go. He grinned at me, but the smile did not reach his eyes. I decided then that he was more of a snake than a cat.

After I'd called at the station to let them know about the van at Mrs Marrick's, I decided to go home for lunch. I needed some time alone.

When I entered the cottage, I heard voices in the sitting room. 'It was just the way she said it,' Annabel was saying. 'I wouldn't have bothered you both with it, but it made me think.'

'I said it was stupid!' That was Leo's voice.

'Or deliberate,' said Tom.

14

I pushed open the sitting room door and saw Annabel, Tom, and Leo all standing there, deep in discussion. As soon as they saw me, they stopped and looked at me in a strange way. What were they suggesting?

'Hello, sweetie,' said Annabel. 'I thought you were at work.'

'I came home for lunch. What's all this? How to solve the problem of stupid Bobbie? I can assure you I did not get shot deliberately!'

'Of course not, darling,' said Annabel, coming across and throwing her arms around me as if she had not seen me for years. Then Tom hugged me and called me his 'darling sister'. Finally Leo put his arms around me and held on to me tightly, as if nothing had happened between us that morning. I was too taken aback to argue.

'We're going to the pub for lunch, sweetheart,' Leo said. 'We were just waiting for you.'

'You didn't know I'd be coming home.'

'Yes, we did,' said Annabel, clearly lying through her teeth. They could not have been expecting me at all. 'Well, I guessed you would come home. You had that 'I'm coming home for lunch' look on your face this morning. Let's get to the pub before all the pies go, shall we?'

I followed them mutely, wondering what on earth they had been talking about that they would not discuss with me. But I let it go, because when you have felt as though the whole world is against you, it's possible to feel pathetically grateful when people start to like you again. I think that was me on that day when we reached the pub. I had not had much time to think of the ramifications of their secret discussion, so I was willing to take their affections at face value.

I was everyone's darling Bobbie again, and I must confess that my ego quite enjoyed that state of affairs without wondering too much what had brought it about. Leo kept holding my hand and smiling at me with big sad puppy-dog eyes. Annabel and Tom fussed about fetching me a pie and a half-pint of lager and lime.

'How are your investigations going, Bobbie?' Tom asked when we had finished eating.

'I found out from the old files that Mrs Marrick over at Little Stony was injured the last time the bank was robbed,' I explained. 'I've just been to speak to her, but she's being a bit vague about it all.'

'Clever girl,' said Tom. OK, adoration I could cope with, but patronisation was a bit galling. I let it slide. I was just happy to be in everyone's good graces again.

'She didn't tell me much,' I said, 'but the M.O. appears to be the same.'

'M.O.?' asked Annabel.

'Modus operandi,' I said, secretly pleased that I knew something she did not. Yes, my ego was flying rather high. I half-expected to be burned by the sun. I might also have been mixing up my metaphors and Greek gods. 'They wore masks, but these were of Bob Hope, Bing Crosby, and Dorothy Lamour. Or it might have been Carmen Miranda.'

'Oh, I love those old 'Road to' films,' said Annabel.

'Me too,' said Tom.

'I've got some up at the house,' Leo chimed in. 'My father used to buy old stock from the cinemas. We should make an evening of it sometime. Dinner for four, then a night of Bing and Bob. What do you say, Bobbie?' He seemed to have taken Annabel and Tom's coupling as a fait accompli even before I did.

'Yes, if you like.'

'Anyway,' Tom said, 'you were saying?' He looked at me expectantly.

'That's it. They hit Mrs Marrick and she gave them the combination. I know it was the right thing for her to do, but something about it feels wrong.'

'That's interesting,' said Tom. 'Is there

any connection between Mrs Marrick and Mr Preston?'

'Not as far as I know. She left the bank soon after the war. Or during. That bit was fuzzy, because Miss Hooper was going to correct her, but then she didn't. Mrs Marrick must have seen Mr Preston in the bank if and when she went in, but they don't live near to each other, and as far as I know they didn't socialise. I never thought to ask. Her son is an odd one, though. He dodged the draft during the war.'

'No!' Annabel exclaimed. She, Tom, and Leo were also children of their time. It was as shocking to them as it had been to me.

'Is there anything else you might have found out?' asked Tom.

'What do you mean? From Mrs Marrick? That's about it. Oh, there's an old van that's turned up in her garage. I presume it belongs to Alan Marrick. There's something about him I don't quite trust.'

'When did you see the van?' asked Leo.

'This morning.'

'Nothing else before that?' Tom asked. 'On your travels. Talking to locals and all that.'

'No. I'm sorry, Tom. No one has let me do much of the question-asking.'

'No, of course not, love. No one is blaming you. I only wondered if there was something you knew but didn't know you knew.'

'Well if I don't know I know something, how can I tell you what it is?'

'Fair enough, sis. I really meant anything that you'd overheard or seen that seemed like nothing but might be something important.'

'Well . . . there's been someone standing in the lane outside the cottage late at night.'

'Who?' Leo cut in.

'I don't know. I thought it was you one night, but when I called your name, he walked away. I've not seen his face.'

'Bobbie, why didn't you report it to the police, sweetie?' asked Annabel.

'Because I *am* the police, so it

seemed daft to ring them. Whoever it is hasn't done anything other than stand there smoking a cigarette. It could just be someone out for a walk. I only mention it because you said to tell you anything I've seen but dismissed as nothing. Anyway, why are you asking me this? We have witnesses to the bank robbery. Both bank robberies. I wasn't there at the time; I was up at Mrs Marrick's, about her break in. Only, it wasn't a break in. It was her son, who'd turned up and then left without leaving a note. He's a very selfish man.'

'I'm only trying to draw on your expertise of local people, Bobbie,' said Tom. 'Didn't you say I should?'

'Yes, well yes, of course.'

'What about that Mrs Higgins? I still think she was harbouring young Clyde Smith.'

'Oh no,' Annabel interrupted. 'No, Tom. She wouldn't. I mean yes, she might help Clyde. She's kind like that. In her very strange way. But she wouldn't . . . wouldn't . . . '

'Get involved in a bank robbery?' I suggested. I laughed. 'I'm not so sure about that. Apparently she worked for the resistance in the war. But no, of course she wouldn't get involved in a bank robbery,' I added, afraid that Tom might go straight to Mrs Higgins's caravan and arrest her. 'Anyway,' I said to Tom, 'what have you got?'

'Not much. Mr Preston's death left us without one major source of information.'

'Did you speak to Mr Otterburn?'

'Oh yes,' Tom said, laughing. 'He's very, erm . . . feminine. In fact . . . ' Tom leaned in and spoke in a low voice. 'Old Mr Otterburn has got a record for obscene behaviour.'

'What did he do?' I asked. 'I know about Mr Watson. He's got a telescope and claims to be a stargazer, but he's often just watching women undress through their windows, and he flashed one lady in the park.'

'Not that sort of obscene behaviour,' Tom said. 'He's . . . you know. A homosexual. And quite obviously so.'

'Really?' I sat back, trying to remember something that had made me stop and think only recently. Whatever it was had escaped from me. 'Poor man.'

'It's illegal, Bobbie,' said Tom.

'I know, but a lot of people think it shouldn't be illegal. And well, he can't help it, can he?'

'It causes a lot of problems,' said Leo.

'What?' I asked. 'Health problems?'

'No, not health problems.' AIDS was unheard of back then. I often wish it still was. 'But it does leave the men open to blackmail.'

'Oh,' I said, sitting up straight, the germ of an idea forming. I had remembered what it was I had noticed. 'Tom, have you checked that Mr Otterburn really is Mr Preston's cousin?'

'No, I hadn't thought of it.'

'Perhaps we should. Because something has been wrong about this robbery all along.'

'What?'

'I don't know for certain yet, but I'll tell you when I do know.'

'OK, we'll find out.'

'Anyway, what have you found out, Mr Scotland Yard man?' I teased. 'You're supposed to be the experts.'

'Well, Miss Stony End woman, we've found out that some of the fingerprints at that derelict cottage belong to a certain Jimmy Ogden. Carl and some of the constables have gone looking for him now.'

'Really? Have you checked on his father too — William Ogden? They've done some stuff together in the past.'

'Have they? I'll get on it.'

'Any news on who owns the land the derelict cottage is on?'

'Well it used to belong to a certain Leo Stanhope,' said Tom with a grin.

'You robbed the bank?' I said to Leo. 'Is this another one of those secrets I should know about?' I was in a calm enough mood to joke again.

'You got me bang to rights, Guv,' said Leo. 'Except I was at the hospital, helping a woman to give birth, with Annabel as my witness, when the most recent robbery took place.'

'Yes, he was,' Annabel agreed.

'You could be in on it together,' I quipped. 'The Bonnie and Clyde of Stony End.'

'Anyway,' Leo continued, ignoring me but smiling anyway, 'my trustees sold the land during the war. It went to some holding company. I think Tom is trying to find the source — right, Tom?'

'Yes, it's one of those companies within companies. That's often a sign of dodgy dealing. We'll get to know who owns it soon. But that might mean nothing. It's a derelict cottage with easy access. Anyone could have used it. We'll get the names out of Jimmy Ogden with any luck.'

'Come down hard on him?' I said, my mood dropping a little.

'I won't hurt him, Bobbie,' Tom promised.

It was time for me to return to work. Leo walked me to the station. 'Are we OK?' he asked as we walked hand in hand.

'I think so,' I replied.

'Because you know that I have more respect for you than any woman . . . no, not just any woman; than any *person* I have ever met, Bobbie.'

'Do I know that, Leo?'

He stopped and took me by the shoulders, turning me to face him. 'You should know it.'

'Sometimes the things you say . . . '

'What things?'

'Well, that my job isn't good enough for Joe, for a start.'

Leo sighed. 'Bobbie, listen to me. I've had Joe's mother writing to me from prison every week for the last year. She has a clear plan for her son's education. I have been trying to respect her wishes. You know what she sacrificed for her son. When I told her that Joe wanted to join the police, she went crazy. I mean crazier than she normally is. She blames the police for every bad thing that's ever happened to her. There's certainly no personal responsibility there. I've had to balance what she wants against what Joe wants, and it's hard, because I want the kid to be happy. When I told him he could do better, it's because his mother had been nagging me to make sure he went to university. I can't blame her for wanting that for her son, even if I don't agree with her stance on the police.'

'Well, it's a reason, though I'm not convinced it's all coming from Joe's mother.'

'It is, I promise. The work you do is incredibly important, and you are a fantastic policewoman.'

'Despite my stupidity?'

'I didn't call you stupid, Bobbie. I said the situation was stupid. I'm sorry you took it the wrong way. I was so worried about you that for a while I couldn't really remember what I'd said at the time. Then I was reminded today because . . . well, that doesn't matter.'

'You have such a way of using logic to get out of trouble, Leo Stanhope. I really shouldn't trust you at all.'

'But you do?'

'Remember when we wondered if we would ever find our song?'

'I remember.'

'Sometimes I still don't think we've found it. We're so out of tune that sometimes the noise hurts. Especially now I've got a poorly ear.' Me and my metaphors!

'If everything were perfect, we'd have nothing worth fighting for, Bobbie. We'd get complacent and bored.'

'But does love have to be such a struggle all the time? I look at Annabel and Tom, who have just got through it all easily. And I'm so tired . . . '

'I know, darling. Me too.'

I stroked his cheek. 'We will find our song, won't we?'

'I believe it's out there, waiting for us.'

15

Jimmy Ogden was arrested that afternoon. He had been trying to buy a ferry ticket to the continent. A lot of ex-cons were heading for Spain, and it seemed that he hoped to join them. Tom and Carl brought him in. He swaggered into the police station with a cigarette tucked behind his ear, the pack rolled into his T-shirt sleeve.

'You've got nothing on me,' he said at the reception desk as I booked him into a cell.

'We've got your fingerprints all over a cottage that we believe was used by the bank robbers,' said Tom.

'So? Me and the lads go up there sometimes, to drink and play cards. It's not illegal.'

'It is if you're trespassing,' said Carl.

I finished booking Jimmy in, and half-hoped that Tom and Carl would let me sit in on the interrogation, but apparently that was too much to ask. 'Fetch Jimmy a cup of tea, please, WPC Blandford,' Tom said.

'OK.' I made the tea and went into the interrogation room, just in time to see Tom slamming his fist down in such a way that the table jumped, but so did Jimmy . . . and me. I almost dropped the cup. Luckily Tom only hit the table, but I feared things could get worse.

'Give us the other names, Jimmy.'

'You've got no proof I was involved.'

'That Electrolux cooker your mother just bought was a bit expensive, wasn't it?' Carl asked in his mild way. 'She doesn't earn that much at the bank.'

'She got it on the never ever,' Jimmy said. The 'never ever' was local slang for hire purchase, the joke being that people didn't really intend to pay for the goods.

'We've seen the receipt,' said Tom. 'She paid cash.'

'Maybe she's been saving up. I don't know how she buys things.'

'She must have been saving quite a while . . . Thanks, Bobbie,' said Tom, finally realising I was in the room. 'Leave it on the table.'

I put the cuppa in front of Jimmy and really wanted to hang around. Tom seemed to behave better when I was there. I had no choice but to leave them. I stood outside the door for a while, but could only hear the hum of voices. Nothing was clear enough, apart from the occasional word spat out by Tom, some of which were not fit to repeat. I did not like it at all. I could only hope that Carl would be a calming influence.

An hour later, I put Jimmy into his cell for the night. He was swaggering a little less and was clearly exhausted by all the questions.

'I did nothing,' he said to me, but he sounded less sure.

'Just tell them, Jimmy,' I said. 'Make it easier for yourself.'

'I'm no snitch, right?'

'I understand that, but an innocent man has died. Surely you didn't want that to happen.'

'Nothing to do with me. Anyway, he wasn't that innocent by all accounts.'

'Who did hit him? If it wasn't you, then you won't be in as much trouble.'

'I've told you, I've nothing to say. 'Specially not to a woman.'

'Did you get anything out of him?' I asked Tom mildly when I went back to the kitchen. Tom and Carl had made themselves a cup of coffee each. I wanted to talk to my brother about his behaviour, but felt stifled by Carl being there.

'Nothing,' said Tom. 'I'll say this for Jimmy — he's no snitch.'

'That's what he's just said. You should find his father,' I suggested. 'William Ogden. They were arrested together a couple of years ago. Mrs Ogden makes out that he didn't come back from the war, but he's got a record as long as your arm.'

'Maybe that's something you could do, Bobbie,' Carl suggested. 'Go and speak to her and find out the truth about that.'

'Yes! Great!' I was more than happy to do my bit.

'Good idea,' said Tom. 'I'm going to go and check out that van up at Mrs Marrick's house. I'll get a cast of the tyres. It might be nothing, but Bobbie's instincts have been good so far. Carl, can you take care of things here?'

I felt a few inches taller, receiving such praise from the brother I idolised.

'No problem,' Carl agreed.

I had to wait until the bank closed before I could speak to Mrs Ogden. She had no idea, until I told her, that her son had even been arrested. She was so upset that I accompanied her home and made her a cup of tea. I had to wait until she was calmer before I could ask questions, but it turned out I did not need to. She seemed happy to get things off her chest.

'He's just like his father,' she sniffed, wiping her nose with a handkerchief. 'Bill was always getting into trouble. That's why we had to leave our other house.'

'I thought, from what you had said, that William — Bill — had died in the war.'

'I let people believe that. The truth was that he spent much of the war in prison. Jimmy was conceived during one of the few times he was out. I thought it was romantic when I first met him . . . Bill, I mean. He was one of those bad boys young girls are always warned about. But I couldn't put up with his criminal ways and I didn't want Jimmy brought up like that.' Her voice lacked conviction. I got the impression that she did not entirely disapprove of her husband's lifestyle.

'Did you know that Jimmy was amongst the men who robbed the bank?'

'No, he was not!' Mrs Ogden's eyes flared at me. 'He was not.'

'Clyde Smith wasn't there, was he?'

'Perhaps not. I don't know.'

'So why did you say he was?'

'Well he's . . . what does it matter? I probably made a mistake. It doesn't matter for his sort, does it? He's got a prostitute for a mother and a black man for a father. He's probably a criminal anyway.'

'Clyde Smith is innocent.' I decided to change tack as I could not stomach any more of Mrs Ogden's racism. 'How did you afford your new cooker?'

'I bought it on hire purchase.'

'No, you didn't. We checked with the Co-op. You paid cash. You lied to me about Clyde being at the bank. You've now lied to me about your cooker. What else have you lied about, Mrs Ogden? Did you do it to protect Jimmy? Was that it?'

'Thank you for letting me know my son has been arrested, WPC Blandford. I don't think I have any more to say to you.'

'If you had a part in this, Mrs Ogden, then it will be found out. Even if you only received stolen goods. So the more you can tell me, the better it might be for you.'

'I'm a respectable woman.'

'You're a woman who wants whatever

her neighbours have. Is that how you got involved with Bill? Did he promise you all the things you'd never had?'

'I am a respectable woman.'

'OK, one last question. Did you know that Mr Preston was a homosexual?'

'What?' She almost laughed at that. I think she was relieved that I'd moved away from asking about her involvement in the bank robbery. 'Well, I suppose we all did. He was so fastidious. I . . . a friend of mine saw something in his diary. Well, it was obvious then that they were not cousins.'

'What friend?'

'Excuse me?'

'What friend read his diary? Could that friend have told Jimmy?'

'I don't remember what friend. I'm sure Jimmy didn't know.'

I realised I was not going to get much more out of Mrs Ogden. She would lie about anything. Whether to protect her son, or herself, I did not know. It was possible that she had read Mr Preston's diary, then dropped it when she realised she might be discovered, leaving Mrs Green to pick it up and get caught. Or Mrs Green read it and passed on the information. They were close friends.

Mrs Green had also said that she believed the bank robbers were two older men and two younger men. If one of the younger men was Jimmy, and the older man his father, that left one older man and one younger man unaccounted for. By then I had a good idea who one of the older men was.

I went back to the station and started making phone calls. I would like to say I got the answers straight away. But people rarely had the answers at their fingertips in those days. There were no computers where all files were at hand. Instead, there were dozens of offices all over the country with underpaid, overworked clerks drowning in paperwork. And that was just recent paperwork. Files going back eighteen years or more were even harder to find. Most police and prison filing systems were not much better than the one I had down in the cellar.

If I had found out the truth sooner, the tragedy might not have happened.

I was getting dressed the next morning when Annabel, who had only just come in off a night shift, called me to the phone. It was supposed to be my day off.

'Blandford,' the sarge barked, 'get to the station now!'

Wondering what trouble I could be in, I jumped on my Vespa and headed for the station, still wearing a V-neck sweater and jeans, unsure if I should have put on my uniform.

There was a strange atmosphere in the station. Normally it was busy, with coppers moving around and people coming in to report stolen or lost property. But a hush had come over the place. Even those coming in from outside seemed to know that they had to be quieter than normal. The air was thick with some unknown emotion and it was infectious, leaving us all feeling sick and worried.

The sarge was waiting for me at his office door, giving me no time to talk to anyone else. 'In here,' he said.

'What's wrong, Sarge?' I asked when he had closed the door. 'What have I done now?'

'I want to know everything that happened yesterday afternoon when you booked Jimmy Ogden.'

'Well, Tom . . . Detective Blandford and Detective Latimer brought him in. They spoke to him for about an hour.'

'Did you see him at all during that hour?'

'Yes, Sarge. I took him a cup of tea.'

'What sort of state was he in?'

'Cocky, arrogant.'

'Had he been injured in any way?'

I hesitated, immediately seeing Tom's fist hitting the table in my mind's eye. 'No, Sarge. He was fine. I mean, he was a bit more subdued after they'd questioned him for an hour, but no one had hurt him as far as I could see. What's happened, Sarge? Has someone hit him?'

He ignored my question. 'Did you see him again after that?'

'Erm . . . Yes, I took him his tea. We got some fish and chips from Dottie's — well not Dottie's now, but — '

'Yes, I know the chippie has changed hands. You got him fish and chips. Go on.'

'Yes, with some bread and butter, and I made him another cuppa. Then I handed over to the night-time desk sergeant. Ernie Turner was on.'

'What sort of state was Ogden in when you took him his food?'

'He was OK, Sarge. He had his food. I think he ate it all right, but then I went home, so it wasn't me who cleared his tray away. What's happened, Sarge?'

'Who was at the station when you left?'

'I can't remember. I mean, Ernie was here . . . '

'Was your brother around?'

It was at this point that my legs began to turn to jelly. 'No, Sarge. I mean, I don't think so. He went up to check on the van at Mrs Marrick's.'

'And he didn't return before you left?'

'No, Sarge. What's going on? Has someone hit Jimmy?'

'It's worse than that, Blandford. He's been badly beaten.'

'Oh God!' I thought about my brother and how desperate he was to solve the case. But would he go that far? 'Is Jimmy in hospital?'

'It was too late for that.'

'What do you mean, Sarge?'

'Jimmy hanged himself in his cell during the night. He's dead.'

16

It sounds dramatic to talk of having a nemesis. I had two of them, and the irony of it was that they were supposed to be on the side of the angels. One was Superintendent Kirkham, who did not like women being in the service, and disapproved of me in particular. This was mainly because I had not allowed him to initiate me by stamping me as 'vermin' on my upper thigh during my first year of probation. My other nemesis was PC Peter Porter, who had once worked at Stony End station, but had been asked to leave after joining in Kirkham's harassment. Since then he had been Kirkham's lap dog.

Both were smirking when they arrived to investigate the death of Jimmy Ogden. 'Why am I not surprised that a Blandford is involved in this?' Kirkham asked.

I bit my tongue. Kirkham would do

anything to shut down the station, so I knew I had to be on my best behaviour.

'We don't know that,' said the sarge. He had called me back into his office to give my version of the events of the night before, along with the night-duty sergeant, Ernie Turner. I had not told the sarge about Tom banging his fist on the table. I still wanted to protect my brother. I had not seen him hit Jimmy, and part of me still wanted to believe he was not capable of such a thing.

Unfortunately, the initial findings of the coroner were not good. It did back up my story about Jimmy having fish and chips for supper, along with a cup of tea. But he had died with two broken ribs, and his jaw had been broken in several places. Someone had really gone to town on him, though it seemed certain that in the end he had died by his own hand. The consensus was that he had committed suicide because he was terrified of what would happen to him.

'Where are Tom Blandford and the

other one? What's his name — Carl Latimer?' asked the superintendent.

'They're off elsewhere today, still investigating this bank robbery,' the sarge explained. 'We haven't had a chance to speak to them.'

'Very well,' said Kirkham. 'WPC Blandford, tell us your version of events. And I will know if you're lying to protect your brother.'

I immediately bristled at the idea that Kirkham automatically thought I would lie to save Tom. But would I, if I really believed Tom had harmed Jimmy in such a way? I wanted to be loyal to my brother, but the part of me that had joined the police force to ensure justice felt differently. Things were not supposed to happen that way. We were supposed to gather evidence and get confessions by legal means, not terrorise a young man into killing himself. Jimmy Ogden might only have been lovable to his mother, but he was still a human being.

I went through my story again, stumbling a little over the part where I took tea into the interview room.

'Were they hitting him?' asked Kirkham.

'No, sir, they were not.' That at least was the truth.

'Were they being aggressive?'

'Erm . . . yes, sir. In their language and the way they questioned him. But no differently to — '

'So they *were* being aggressive.'

'But it was within the parameters of what's allowed. Sometimes we have to be a bit tougher with people to — '

'I don't need you to tell me what's allowed, Blandford. I already know that. Is that all you can tell us?'

'Yes, sir.'

'Right. Ernie, you're an experienced duty sergeant.'

Straight away, it was obvious that Kirkham was going to be much softer on Ernie than he had been on me. Ernie was addressed by his first name, for a start.

'I like to think so, sir.'

'What happened after WPC Blandford left?'

'It was a quiet night, sir,' said Ernie. 'I checked on the prisoners regularly, as it says in the handbook. I cleared away Jimmy's tray. He'd eaten all his food and drank his tea. He was in good spirits then. A bit quieter than usual, but not unhappy that I could see.'

'Of course. Did anyone come to see the dead prisoner?'

'I'm not sure, sir. See, I nipped out about two o'clock this morning for a . . . ' Ernie glanced at me and decided to be delicate. 'To go to the toilet. And have a fag.' He looked sheepish.

'Quite right, quite right. You're entitled to a break. How long were you gone?'

I wondered what would have been said if I'd left the desk unattended to go on a break.

'No more than five minutes, sir.'

I doubled and even tripled that time in my head. No one could go to the loo and smoke a cigarette in five minutes, and I knew Ernie well enough to know that his breaks often lasted longer than they should.

'Is it possible someone came in whilst you were in the loo?'

'Only if they had a key, sir. We lock the door at night.'

'Did the Scotland Yard men have a key?' Kirkham asked the sarge.

'Yes, sir. I gave one to Detective Blandford, just in case they needed to bring a suspect in during the night.'

'I see,' said Kirkham.

'That doesn't mean anything,' I protested. 'Tom wouldn't do this.' Even as I said it, I heard the lack of conviction in my own voice.

'Thank you, Blandford,' said Kirkham. 'You're hardly an uninterested party here. When you returned, Ernie, when did you next check the prisoners?'

'Straight away of course, sir,' said Ernie.

'What was Jimmy Ogden doing?'

'He was asleep.'

'Did you see his face?'

'No, sir. He was facing the wall. But I asked him if he was all right and he said yes. I think he might have been crying a bit. But that's normal for prisoners, when it gets quiet and they reflect on their situation.'

I glanced at Ernie, and noticed the tips of his ears were very pink. He was lying! I wondered for a moment if he had decided to try and crack the case himself by giving Jimmy a drubbing, but I had known Ernie for three years. He might be liable to leave the desk for longer than necessary to go for a cuppa and a cigarette, but he was not a violent man.

'Well,' said Kirkham, 'there's little we can do until Tom Blandford and the other one come back. I want to make it clear, Sergeant Simmonds, that we will not allow this sort of behaviour in one of our police stations.'

I almost said, 'No, but you don't mind branding a woman as vermin whilst your lap dog holds her down,' but I thought better of it. Besides, as much as I disliked Kirkham, he was only doing his job, and he was right to mount a thorough investigation into

Jimmy's death. I just doubted that it had anything to do with getting justice for Jimmy, and more to do with Kirkham's pleasure at finding an excuse to punish a Blandford and shut down Stony End station.

I was sent home for the rest of the day, since I was not supposed to be on duty anyway, but told to be ready to come in at a moment's notice. Annabel was at home when I returned to the cottage, having managed to get a rare afternoon off. We had been supposed to go shopping together in the big town, but I was no longer in the mood. Neither was Annabel when I told her about Jimmy.

'His poor mother,' she said.

'Annabel, it's worse than that. They think Tom hurt him.'

'No, Bobbie. Tom wouldn't do that!' Annabel blushed prettily. It was obvious she really liked my brother, but how well did she even know him? I was not sure *I* knew him anymore, and yet I had grown up with him.

'He might . . . He was rearing up for

something when he questioned Jimmy yesterday. For God's sake, don't tell the sarge and Superintendent Kirkham that. I've left that little nugget out. I know I should tell, but . . . '

'No, you shouldn't tell, because Tom wouldn't do that. I know I haven't known him long, but he wouldn't.'

'At some time during the night, when Ernie was away from the desk, someone came in and gave Jimmy a good hiding. Then Jimmy hanged himself. It's as good as murder.'

'Well then it wasn't Tom.'

'How do you know?'

Annabel blushed again. 'Because he spent the night with me at a hotel on the Stockport road. He got back from my parents' house about eight last night and we went for dinner, and then . . . well, I don't have to draw you a picture, do I?'

'Annabel!' I did not know whether to laugh or cry. I did almost collapse in relief. 'Really? You and Tom?'

'Why not me and Tom?'

'Oh no, it's wonderful. Two of the people I love most in the world — together. I love it! I just can't help thinking I've been walking around with blinkers on lately.'

'You have had your own problems. Anyway, we haven't advertised the fact. I love him, Bobbie. That's why I know he wouldn't have done this awful thing. He said he was up at Mrs Marrick's yesterday, checking on that van. He's taken a mould of the tyres, and was going to check it today, but he's had to go down to London to talk to his superior officers. He'll be back tonight, and we can sort this out once and for all.'

'But if it wasn't Tom, who was it?'

'There's something else, Bobbie.'

'What?'

'Have a cup of tea first, then I'll tell you.'

'I've done nothing but drink tea at the station all morning. I'm sloshing. Just tell me.'

'You know when you were shot . . . '

'I vaguely remember it on account of

it only being last weekend.'

'The reason Tom went to my parents' house was to ask questions. You see, we — Tom, Leo, and I — think someone shot you deliberately.'

'What? And you didn't think to mention this to me?'

'We didn't want to worry you, sweetie. Especially if we were wrong. But as Leo said, it was all so stupid.'

'He said *I* was stupid.'

'No, sweetie. He said the situation was stupid. You weren't on the shooting range; you were on a perfectly safe path. Of course sometimes these incidents do happen with an inexperienced shooter, but no one there that day was inexperienced. That's why we wondered if you'd seen or heard anything untoward whilst at Mummy and Daddy's. Don't worry if it's about them. You won't offend or shock me. Daddy's been involved in some very silly schemes to make money in the past. Few of them would pass as legal.'

'He was interested in Frobisher's

shares, but buying shares is not illegal, Annabel. Besides . . . Oh . . . '

'What? What is it?'

'I overheard a telephone conversation the night before, coming from the study. I hadn't thought about it because it had nothing to do with anything. Somebody was talking about how the old man hadn't said anything, then something else about shares. I assumed it was something your dad was involved in, because he and Jack Frobisher had been talking about shares at dinner. I didn't hear what the person on the other end said. But what if the conversation was about two separate things? What if the first half was about Mr Preston and the bank robbery, and the second part was about your dad and the shares? Annabel, would you be upset if I contacted the telephone exchange and asked what calls were made on that night? I don't want to drag your mum and dad into this, but . . . '

'Make the call, Bobbie. No one shoots my best friend and gets away with it! Mummy and Daddy will just have to learn to choose their friends more carefully.'

'But I don't know who was talking, Annabel. What if — '

'Sweetie, not five minutes ago you were determined not to let your brother get away with police brutality. What sort of a person would I be if I didn't stand up for justice, even if it does involve Mummy and Daddy? I know Daddy is flat broke. That's why he's so keen for me to marry Jack Frobisher. They have money, though God knows how. Their house leaks cash even more than Daddy's does.'

I rushed back to the station, feeling that any discussions with the telephone exchange would be more official if I contacted them from that number.

'What are you doing back, Blandford?' asked the sarge when he saw me walk in.

I quickly explained to him what I was doing, half-expecting him to tell me to get lost.

'Right, go on then, Blandford. Don't take all day about it.'

'It's all right, Sarge?'

'Your instincts have been good in the past. Even if you're wrong, it won't hurt to ask.'

Things might have taken longer in the '60s, but they were also much easier. We did not have to go through so much red tape and bureaucracy to get information. The Data Protection Act had not come into force, so it was relatively easy to contact a telephone exchange and get the answers you wanted almost immediately. Plus, the operators were not exactly discreet. It was almost impossible to have a secret when all telephone calls had to go through an exchange. There was no direct dial. You had to dial for the operator, then ask her for the number you wanted. She was then supposed to disconnect her end of the call, but that did not always happen. Part of me wondered if that was how information got around Stony End so quickly. Mrs

Braddock at the exchange was rather gossipy, usually starting her conversations with 'I wouldn't tell anyone but you this . . . '

'I'm not sure I can tell you,' said the operator at the Shropshire exchange. I played along with her, understanding that she had to feign reluctance.

'It is a matter of great importance,' I said. 'You could be helping to solve a major crime.'

'Oh, really? Well, of course, I want to do my bit for British justice. Is there a reward?'

There was a reward for the capture of the bank robbers, but I was not sure if she would be eligible, given that she came by any information in the course of her job. I ummed and ahhed, but avoided saying an absolute no.

'It's funny you should have called from Stony End,' she said, once she was satisfied she might get something. 'The call was made through to the Stony End exchange. To a . . . '

I think I knew what name she was

going to say before she said it. Everything began to slot into place. I put the phone down and went to see the sarge.

'Should I put my uniform on, Sarge?' I asked after I had told him my theory.

'No. I think it might help if you go up there in plain clothes. The gentle touch, so to speak. You go on ahead, and I'll send Alf and a couple of the other lads after you, in case there's any trouble.'

I got on my Vespa and rode up to Little Stony, my heart heavy. It was always difficult, if you admired some-one, to have to deal with them on an official basis.

I knocked on the door and she opened it almost immediately.

'I've been expecting you for some time now, Bobbie,' said Mrs Marrick. 'I even wrote you a letter, but I'm glad you came in time for me to explain everything to your face.'

17

'It's almost a relief,' she said when she had shown me into the sitting room and told me to sit down. I looked around me, feeling that something was missing. The house had a strained atmosphere. The sitting room, like the rest of the house, was spotlessly clean, with fresh flowers filling all the vases, and a fire glowing in the hearth.

'Where is Miss Hooper?' I asked.

'Beattie is in bed . . . asleep.'

Something about her tone concerned me. I went to stand up again.

'No!' she snapped, causing me to drop back down quickly. 'No,' she added more gently. 'I need to tell you why.'

'I think I know,' I said. 'But I may have it wrong.'

I wondered if I could rush past her to get upstairs, but she sat next to me, putting herself between me and the only door from the room. Placing her hand on my arm, she practically held me down, despite trying to appear relaxed and unconcerned.

'I was always going to be a wonderful wife,' Mrs Marrick said, her eyes glazed as if she were looking back into the past. 'I had all the skills — cooking, embroidery, cleaning. I was good at it, and I think . . . I hope . . . I made my husband happy. If I sometimes felt as if I could scream at the banality of it all, I told myself that all wives felt this way. Do you know that alcoholism is a major problem for married women? They start having that first glass of sherry earlier and earlier in the day, until finally they only just stop short of pouring it onto their cornflakes. My addiction turned out to be something else entirely. Just before the war, my younger brother brought home his wife-to-be.'

'Beattie Hooper?'

'Yes. She was thirty years old and quite lovely, both in body and spirit. We became the best of friends. And after a while that friendship blossomed into something else. Oh, we both fought it. We'd been brought up to think of such things as mortal sins, even if for us it was not against the law. One never entirely loses that guilt. That fear of what society would say. It is all very well if you run with the bohemian crowd, but we were a long way from that sort of society here in Little Stony. Respectability means everything here. It means everything to us, too. We may have admitted our feelings to each other, but we could never admit them to the world. We cared too much about what people thought of us. They might suspect, but no one would know for sure. There is nothing unusual about two women on a low income sharing a house.'

'Or two men,' I suggested.

Mrs Marrick nodded. 'Yes, or two men. Poor Mr Preston and Mr Otterburn. No one realises how cruel that law is for those who have no choice in how they feel. Where was I? Oh, my husband . . . I think he knew, especially when Beattie called off her engagement to my brother, but he never said anything. He was probably too old to go to war, but he went anyway. Alan believes I drove his father away, and that my husband deliberately went off to war to get killed. It's strange, but it didn't occur to me that Alan knew about me and Beattie. We always think of our children as children, even when they are older.'

'He blackmailed you,' I said.

'Yes. When he was a teenager he fell in with Bill Ogden, young Jimmy's father. They were in prison together. Oh, that poor boy. I know what Jimmy did was wrong, but to die like that . . . '

I shuddered. 'It's terrible. So much loss of life, and all due to greed.'

'I never took anything,' she said emphatically. 'Alan and Bill cooked up this idea of robbing the bank. This was the first time around, during the war. Alan told me that if I didn't help him, he would tell the world about me and Beattie. He even had pictures. God knows how and when he took them . . . I wish I'd been braver. I wish I could have coped with the scandal of our secret coming out. Even if I could, Beattie could not. She seems hardy, but she isn't. Not emotionally. Her mother and father were still alive, and she feared the truth would kill them.'

'What happened at the bank?'

'They came in wearing their masks. Silly things, they were. But Alan and Bill were too well-known around Stony End. If they'd tried stockings, they'd have been recognised. Even then I feared their voices would be known, but the masks muffled them. They found a way to get the manager out of the bank that morning. I told Alan that if I was to help them, he would have to make it look good. That he would have to hit me in front of the other clerks to make it appear I'd been forced into giving out the combination to the safe. I don't think he cared that much. I think he'd been wanting to strike out at me for a long time and this was his chance. I know it hurt . . . ' She rubbed her temple as if still feeling the pain of the cosh. 'I suppose I'll be arrested now.'

'Possibly, yes. Did you know that Mr Preston was a homosexual?'

Mrs Marrick yawned and I wondered for a moment if she was bored with the conversation. Her eyes had a glassy look. 'Yes, but I didn't tell my son and Bill Ogden. I had nothing to do with this latest robbery, I swear. I would never put anyone through what I went through. Mr Preston was a nice, gentle man. I've written all this down for you.' She reached into her apron and took out a sealed envelope. It was addressed to me. 'I wanted you to read it, because I think you're a kind girl. You always seem to be, anyway. I hoped you would understand.'

'I think I do,' I said. 'But what you and Miss Hooper do . . . have done . . . it's not against the law. Not like poor Mr Preston and Mr Otterburn.'

'It's against nature and society's laws, and they are far less forgiving than Her

Majesty's Government, I find.'

It occurred to me then that big girls truly did not cry. They simply hid their pain behind baking, gardening, making jam and behaving as society expected them to. The normality helps to hold back the tears, but is it any wonder that women sometimes go completely mad as Mrs Higgins did? How much harder must it be to pretend to feel something that you do not? I could see by Mrs Marrick's eyes that she had experienced that duplicity, and had only just come out of it with her sanity. And maybe even that was gone . . .

'Let me go to her,' I pleaded quietly.

'It's too late, child. I . . . I took her some cocoa last night. I think she knew, because she drank it all down. Usually she just manages a few sips before falling asleep.'

'Why?' I asked, my eyes filling with tears, thinking of Miss Hooper lying cold in a room above us. 'Why add murder to what you've done? You might have got away with it, because your son clearly blackmailed you into helping.'

'Then what would we do? Where could we go?' She lay against the back of the sofa. That was when I realised she was not bored, but incredibly sleepy. I was torn between leaving the room to telephone for an ambulance and finding out more before it was too late.

'Who was the other man?' I asked. 'Tell me quickly. There were two older men and two younger men. I know that your son and Bill and Jimmy Ogden were involved. Who was the other one?'

'I don't know. It was some upper-class twit who wanted to play at being a bank robber.'

I breathed a sigh of relief. If it was a young man, it would not be Annabel's father. 'Don't you know anything about him? His name?'

She shook her head. 'Alan never said it. I think even he was afraid of it getting out.'

I stood up. 'I'm going to telephone for an ambulance.'

'It's too late, child.'

'Not for Miss Hooper. For you.'

'It's still too late. I made sure of that. I've taken the poison intravenously.' She pulled up her sleeve and showed me the pin prick in the crook of her elbow. 'By the time the ambulance gets here, I'll be dead. I loved her so much, yet I killed her. Now there's nothing left for me.'

Nevertheless, I went to the phone in the hallway and called for an ambulance, then went back to the sitting room and did all I could to revive Mrs Marrick, but to no avail. She slipped away from me.

I went outside where Alf and the others were waiting. 'There's one upstairs and one in the sitting room,' I said before walking across to the garden bench and sitting down. 'But it's too late.'

Seconds later, a black van came screeching from around the back of the house. It moved at such a pace that when it came to turn out of Mrs Marrick's driveway, it veered to the side and crashed into a dry stone wall. They pulled Alan

Marrick and Bill Ogden out of the wreckage, injured but very much alive, each pointing at the other as the murderer.

'What a mess,' said Alf when he had checked inside the house.

18

I cannot pretend that I had very postmodern opinions on homosexuality back then. I have said before that I was a child of my time, and sometimes I had the prejudices of that time, because they were all I knew. But I was always willing to have those attitudes challenged, and to hopefully learn from my mistakes. When you deal with people on a daily basis, and especially with people who are at their worst, whether they're a victim or a criminal, you begin to understand that we are all the same. After what happened with Mrs Marrick and Miss Hooper, I tried to understand better that when two people fall in love, it does not matter what the law books or society says. Love is an overriding force. It defies logic or morality.

Sometimes love can lead to a darkness that also defies logic, as I was

271

to learn when I travelled back from Little Stony that day. My head was heavy with the weight of grief. I had not known Mrs Marrick and Miss Hooper well, but I had liked them. They had been hardworking women who never asked anyone else for anything. In many ways I envied them. Their love had been very complicated indeed, in the climate in which we lived, yet they had survived it together. They might have grown old together very happily, but the evil that others do had led to their sad deaths.

I reached the crossroads in Stony End, when Carl Latimer pulled up alongside me in a black Zephyr. 'Bobbie,' he said, rolling down his window. 'You're just the person I wanted to see.'

'I'm in a hurry, Carl. They've just arrested Alan Marrick and Bill Ogden.'

'So I've heard. I'm told there's a fourth man missing. I thought that if we went up to the old cottage on the Stockport Road, we might find some clues to him. It's easier to know what you're looking for when you have half the story.'

'Yes, that's true. Shall I tell them at the station that you're on your way there?'

'I hoped you'd come with me. Come on, Tom is going to meet us up there. You deserve to be in on this collar as much as anyone.'

'I'm really tired, Carl. It's been a gruelling day.'

'Yes, I heard about Mrs Marrick and Miss Hooper. I'm so sorry. It's a tragedy, Bobbie, but we must carry on, if only for their sakes. Why don't you leave your Vespa here, and I'll drive? Tom's waiting.'

I can only put it down to my low mood that I agreed to go with him. I was too exhausted to argue, and part of me did want to find the fourth man, though I already had a good idea who it was.

I left my Vespa parked in a layby and got into the Zephyr with Carl. 'I ought to radio in and tell them where I am,' I said. I saw Mrs Higgins across the road and absent-mindedly waved to her.

'Already done it whilst you were parking your moped,' he said.

'Oh, thanks.' I think this was when the first little warning note sounded, but I had no good reason to disbelieve him. 'How is Tom?' I asked. 'Has he said anything about Jimmy Ogden's death?'

'Only that the little runt deserved it . . . not that I agree,' Carl added quickly.

'It doesn't sound like the sort of thing Tom would say.' But I no longer knew what my brother might say or do. I knew that he was in love with Annabel, but I was under no illusions that the love of a good woman might stop my brother if he had already stepped over into the darkness.

'You've seen how much pressure he's been under, Bobbie. We both saw how he reacted to Jimmy yesterday, when you brought in the tea — slamming his fist on the table. It's been really worrying me. I'm a good copper, and I believe in fair play with the prisoners, but Tom . . . I know he's your brother, Bobbie, but he's a bad 'un.'

'No,' I said emphatically. 'No, he isn't. I don't believe it.'

'Hey . . . ' Carl put his hand on my knee, and I almost jumped out of the car. 'Sorry.'

'No, it's fine. I'm a bit stressed out myself at the moment. It was awful watching Mrs Marrick die in front of me.'

'You've got a good heart, Bobbie. Just be careful people don't take advantage of it.'

'I like to think I can tell if someone is leading me on.' How those words came back to bite me in the next hour.

'Like Leo, you mean?' Carl sounded doubtful.

'What about Leo? What are you saying?'

'Nothing. Only, Annabel said you'd been with Leo for three years now.'

'Not quite three years.'

'And he hasn't proposed.'

'It was a bit difficult, considering that for part of the time he thought he was married to someone else.'

'And you really want someone who would marry some slut from America after knowing her for twenty-four hours?'

I felt uncomfortable with the way Carl described Leo's almost wife, Cindy-Lou. Whatever I might think of her and the trick she tried to play on Leo, I did not like hearing another woman described in such disparaging terms. 'It wasn't like that. I mean, he was young and he'd been drinking.'

'Well, at least he hasn't made that mistake with you. He's obviously taking his time to make sure.'

'Me and Leo are fine,' I said crisply. I did not like the way the conversation was going, so for the rest of the journey, when Carl spoke, I only answered in monosyllables. The sooner we got to the cottage and Tom was there, the better.

But Tom was not there when we arrived. 'He must have got held up,' Carl said.

'What are we looking for?' I asked, trying to act professional even though my heart was beating rapidly. Carl had given me no reason to fear him, and yet I was afraid. There was something different about him. He seemed less diffident; more sure of himself. In any other man the arrogance might have been attractive, but in Carl, who had seemed so quiet and unassuming, it unnerved me.

'Proof of the fourth man,' he said.

'It sounds like the Cambridge spy ring or a film,' I said lightly, trying to hide how uncomfortable I felt. I told myself I was being silly; that there was nothing wrong with Carl. I'd had a traumatic day, that was all. 'Starring Orson Wells, of course,' I added.

'That was *The Third Man.*'

'Yes, I know that. I was just . . . It was a joke.'

He smiled. 'I love your sense of humour, Bobbie.'

You could have fooled me, I thought. *You don't even get my jokes.* 'I think I know who the fourth man is,' I said. 'We just need proof.' I began searching through broken cupboards and under tables, but I can't say that I really saw anything. I was too busy working out how I could get Carl to take me back to the station without making too big a thing of it.

'Who do you think it is?'

'Jack Frobisher. He's a friend of Annabel's family. I think I overheard him on the phone when I was there. Then Mrs Marrick mentioned some toff who wanted to play at being a bank robber.'

'So that's why he shot you.'

'What?' I turned around so quickly, I caught my bad ear on an open cupboard door. An excruciating pain shot through me, causing my vision to blur. I put my hand to my head and steadied myself on the kitchen table. 'How do you know he shot me?'

'I saw him.'

'What are you saying, Carl? You weren't there that weekend.'

'I've been everywhere that you've been

lately, Bobbie. Haven't you noticed? I've been standing under your bedroom window. I know you've seen me, and you must have wanted me there because you didn't tell me to go away.'

Stupid, stupid, stupid, I thought to myself. I should have telephoned the police. If any other woman had told me a strange man had been outside her house late at night, that's what I'd have told her to do. Yet I didn't, because I *was* the police, and it had seemed ridiculous to call my colleagues out. I was also afraid that if it had been nothing, they would have held me up to ridicule. 'Why would you do that, Carl?'

'It's obvious. I think you're wonderful, Bobbie, and I know you feel the same way about me.'

'I don't feel anything about you, Carl. I love Leo.'

'But he doesn't love you! You know that. That's why you've been so unhappy lately.'

How Carl managed to tap into my secret insecurities, I do not know, but there seemed to be sense in what he said. 'Even if Leo doesn't love me, I love him. I have no interest in you. Now I think we should end this conversation and return to the station.'

Carl slapped his hand down on the table in much the same way Tom had done the day before. 'You're not leaving this place, Bobbie. Not until you admit how you feel.'

'Carl, I've barely said two words to you. How can you translate that into love?'

'Because I knew, the moment I saw you, that you were the one. Do you know how hard I've tried to be the man you need me to be? Even though Tom has been goading me, trying to trick me.'

'Trick you? How?'

'Oh, I know his game. Acting like he's all tough with the prisoners, hoping to catch me out. Trying to discredit me with you. Well, I've changed now, and I've done it for your sake.'

'Where were you last night, Carl? Tell me.'

He looked away. 'I can't remember.'

'Yes, you can. Did you have the station keys from Tom? It's very important to our . . . our relationship that you're honest with me, Carl.'

'Didn't need them. Ernie Turner let me in. I told him I'd seen his wife with some Frenchman outside the pub. Some of the lads told me that story in the kitchen one day. He couldn't leave quickly enough. That left me time enough alone with Jimmy. We try so hard to keep the law, and idiots like him laugh at us. I told Jimmy that if he told on me, I'd make sure he had a really good time in prison. I told that black kid the same when you and Tom went out of the room. That sort are cowards. They soon give in.'

'Jimmy was innocent until proven guilty, and you made him kill himself!'

'He was not innocent. You've proved that.'

'That's not the point, Carl! We have to go through the process. We have to abide by the law. Otherwise, what is the point of us? We might just as well let vigilantes roam the streets.'

'How many guilty men have you seen walk free, Bobbie? How many have solicitors and barristers who can get them off a murder charge?'

'I doubt Jimmy Ogden was that well connected,' I argued.

'He wasn't, but Frobisher is.'

'How did you see him shoot me? How did you come to be in Shropshire?'

'I followed you there, of course. I knew you'd want me near. Only, I couldn't get near because Leo wouldn't leave you alone. I saw Frobisher turn towards you with his gun. Everyone else was too absorbed in what they were doing to notice. I wanted to run to you when you fell, but Leo and your brother got there first. They were the worst few moments of my life, thinking you were dead.'

'Why didn't you come forward afterwards and say you saw him?'

'Haven't we just discussed this? He would have got away with it. Now he hasn't.'

'What do you mean, Carl? What have you done?'

'He won't threaten you any more, darling.' Carl made a move towards me, but I backed away, only to find the kitchen worktop behind me. 'And you don't have to worry about me. Everyone will think Tom did it. He was there last night.'

I did not tell him that Tom had been with Annabel. 'You expect me to let you frame my own brother? How mad are you?' The question was rhetorical, because Carl was quite clearly insane. His reasoning defied logic, because his mind could not see that what he had done was wrong.

'You love me, Bobbie. You'd never do anything to hurt me. We're in it together.'

'We are in nothing together! You're a murderer! Both of Jack Frobisher and Jimmy Ogden!'

'Jimmy Ogden killed himself.'

'You did everything but tie the rope for him, Carl! You drove him to suicide with your threats. And dear God, I've seen enough of death the last couple of days to last me a lifetime.'

'When you've had time to calm down, you'll see that I did everything for the best.'

'Then I hope you'll agree that when I turn you in it will be for the best. Do you think that Jack Frobisher's father, who's a peer of the realm, will think his son deserved to die? Do you think that Mrs Ogden will agree that her son deserved to die?'

'You're talking about a man who shot you, Bobbie. And a kid who would have ended up spending most of his life in prison anyway.'

'It doesn't matter. Don't you see? It doesn't matter what they did. I've sworn to uphold the law, and that includes treating the people we arrest with due respect, regardless of what they've done.'

'You really are naive and stupid, Bobbie. You think that everything is solved by tea and cake,' Carl scoffed. 'That's not the world we live in. It's brutal and dark out there.'

'I know what the world is like. We're not that blinkered in Stony End. We've seen our fair share of evil. That doesn't mean we have to be the same.'

'Darling, listen to us. We've had our first row.'

'I am not your darling, and if you think I'm going to let you frame my brother for your crimes, you've got another think coming.'

'Leo, then. We can say it was him.'

I almost laughed, but I was too frightened. 'No, not Leo either. I'm going back to the police station.'

Of course he blocked my way, catching me by my shoulders, then throwing me back across the kitchen. An old chair collapsed beneath me, and I scrambled to grab hold of something. Carl came over to me. 'Now look what you've made me do. It's your fault, Bobbie. If you'd just understand me.'

'I understand you're a lunatic,' I said. 'And a murderer.'

'No!' He caught hold of me again,

but I was ready for him. Or at least I thought I was. I brought up one of the broken legs of the chair and smashed him on the head with it, but it was so riddled with woodworm that it exploded like a papier-mâché stick. He grabbed my arms and pulled me up, trying to force his lips against mine.

'No!' I screamed. 'Get off me.' I dug my nails into his face, leaving long, deep scratches. Ever the policewoman, I had the vague idea that if I was found dead, they'd be able to get his blood type from my nails.

'You little . . . ' He swore at me then, calling me all the nasty names under the sun. So much for being in love with me! Leo would never have called me those names, and it only deepened my love for him. I wished he was there, but I knew I had to save myself from Carl.

The fight seemed to go on forever, but it was actually only a few seconds. I scratched and bit him, but it only seemed to arouse him, which was not the effect I wanted. 'I hate you,' I said, scratching his face again. 'You're a bully and a pig! You give police a bad name!' I brought up my knee and managed to catch him squarely in the groin, causing him to kneel back, groaning in agony.

Then, just as I thought Carl was going to hit me, he flew backwards. The kitchen was getting dark, so it took me a moment to realise others were there — Tom, Leo, and the sarge.

'Bobbie, darling . . . ' I fell into Leo's arms and he kissed me all over my face. 'Oh God, darling, you were so brave.'

Tom and the sarge had hold of Carl. My brother looked at his former friend murderously. 'You hurt my sister,' he hissed.

'He killed Jack Frobisher,' I said. 'And he drove Jimmy Ogden to suicide.'

'Yes, we know,' said the sarge. 'We've been listening.'

'You couldn't have come in sooner?' I asked.

'We needed to know everything, Blandford, and you did a good job of getting it all out of him. We did have to hold Dr Stanhope back a bit.'

'I take it I'm no longer held back,' said Leo.

'No, you're free to do what you want,' said the sarge.

'Good.' Leo let go of me and turned to Carl. 'You seem to like police brutality. So try some of this.' He raised his fist and socked Carl in the jaw.

It's amazing how I could be a pacifist one moment, and then find it thrilling that the man I loved had thumped my assailant. Leo was just about to go in for another punch, but Tom, the sarge and I held him back.

'You saw that,' Carl said to Tom and the sarge. 'He assaulted a police officer.'

'Did he?' said the sarge. 'I saw nothing.' He turned to my brother. 'What about you, Blandford?'

'Not a thing, Sergeant Simmonds. The prisoner hurt himself when he fell against the table.'

Carl spat some blood from his mouth. 'What happened to all your high ideals?'

'I lost mine years ago having to deal with thugs like you,' said Tom. 'But luckily Bobbie has enough high ideals for all of us.'

'Oh yes,' I said, ashamed that I'd rather enjoyed seeing Leo smack Carl in the kisser. 'Of course I do. But I didn't see anything either.'

On the way back to the station, Tom explained why he'd been behaving the way he had. I travelled with Leo and Tom, whilst the sarge and one of the constables took Carl. Tom drove, and Leo sat in the back seat with me.

'I've been working undercover for Internal Affairs for a while now,' he told me. 'It's our job to root out bent coppers. We'd had some reports of Carl Latimer's violent behaviour, but no one would talk. They were all too afraid. So I became his partner, and I kept trying to goad him into doing something by acting all aggressive myself. But believe me when I say that I only expected him to try to hit a prisoner whilst I was there. I would have put a stop to it

289

immediately. Unfortunately, I think he suspected from the beginning. You didn't help.'

'Thanks very much,' I grumbled.

'I don't mean it that way, sis. But your reaction to my bad behaviour gave away that it was out of character.'

'Why didn't you tell me what you were doing? I'd have reacted in a more helpful way.'

'I couldn't risk Carl finding out. He might have hurt you.'

'Might?'

'OK, he did hurt you. Damn, I wish I had been the one to thump him.'

'It was my pleasure to do it on your behalf,' said Leo.

I put my head on Leo's shoulder. 'All this death, and all for money. I don't get it. We need to find out where Carl killed Jack Frobisher.'

'Frobisher is alive,' Tom said.

'But Carl said he killed him.'

'He tried, but he didn't succeed. Frobisher called the police and he's been put under protection. He thought it was Marrick or Ogden who shot him to cover their tracks. We haven't disabused him of that notion, so he's singing like a canary.'

19

Over the weeks that followed, the papers were full of the story of the bank robbers. They particularly concentrated on the private lives of Mrs Marrick and Miss Hooper, and Mr Preston and Mr Otterburn, eking out the more salacious details. Mr Otterburn had to move away because people started throwing bricks at his windows and hurling abuse at him in the street. They were innocent victims, regardless of Mrs Marrick and Mr Preston giving in to blackmail.

Yet the bank robbers were treated like anti-heroes. Jack Frobisher, by dint of being handsome and a member of the nobility, was particularly popular. Word had it that either Steve McQueen or James Garner was going to play him in an American version of the story.

'It's disgraceful,' I said to Annabel as we read the Sunday papers after a leisurely breakfast. 'Innocent people died. Mr Preston was murdered by Marrick and his friends, yet to read the papers you would think he brought it upon himself because of his sexual preferences. In Mrs Marrick's letter, she makes the point of telling me that she had morals as strong as anyone else. She wanted to be respectable and to be respected. Yet this glitch — that's her word, not mine . . . this love she had for Miss Hooper threatened all that. That's why her son had such a hold over her. I think he was also punishing her for the way she felt. He might have been a crook, but he was very conventional in his sexual morality.'

'He's vile,' said Annabel. 'Doing that to his own mother. I'm still a bit confused about how it all happened. What about the first robbery? There were two other men then, but they can't have been Jimmy Ogden and Jack Frobisher. They were only children at the time.'

'We don't know anything about the other two men in the first robbery. All

Marrick will tell us is that one of them died in prison, but he won't give us a name, presumably because it would identify the other man. Perhaps they were brothers, or related in some way. We don't know, and neither Marrick nor Ogden is saying. Marrick had fallen in with a bad crowd, including Bill Ogden, though I don't think he needed much leading astray. These were mostly young men who had not been called up to go to war. When Mrs Marrick started working at the Stony End bank, Marrick saw his chance, as long as he could get her on his side. He knew she would never help willingly, so he black-mailed her with some photographs he had managed to get of her and Miss Hooper being intimate.'

'The swine!'

'I know! He's truly odious. The idea was that Mrs Marrick would make things easy for them during the robbery. They got the manager out of the way by call-ing to say he was needed in the Home Guard. The robbers made a show of acting violently towards Mrs Marrick, then she let them into the safe. I think that under other circumstances, she might not have done. She was a very honest woman, and I think that if the robbers hadn't had such a hold over her, she would have resisted, even if it cost her life. But she feared that Miss Hooper would be left to deal with the shame. She left her employment at the bank soon afterward, stating that it was the trauma, though she told me in her letter that it was the shame of allowing herself to be blackmailed.

'Flash forward eighteen years, give or take a few months, and Marrick and his friends decide that lightening can strike in the same place twice — especially when Jimmy's mum, Mrs Ogden, went home gossiping about Mr Preston and his 'feminine' ways. She read his diary. The robbers did a bit of searching and found out the truth. They may have had more pictures, but Mr Otterburn is refusing to say. I can't blame him. The poor man has suffered enough abuse.

Anyway, this time Alan Marrick and Bill Ogden had Jimmy Ogden and Jack Frobisher with them.'

'How did Jack become involved?' Annabel asked. 'I knew he was a bit of a tearaway, but this seems wrong for him.'

'He says he was looking for excitement, and a way of filling up the family coffers. Those shares that apparently came good were actually his share of the bank robbery. He's a stupid man. You know the bit about him telephoning Alan Marrick from your parents' house and me overhearing. Apparently he saw me on the stairs and was afraid I'd heard more; hence, shooting at me. It's a good job his rifle skills weren't so good that day.'

'Or maybe he didn't really want to hurt you,' Annabel mused. 'Sorry, but even though I don't want to marry him, I've known him since we were children. Murder seems beyond him. I think it was just a silly chance that he took. Maybe he thought he'd just put you out of action for a while.'

'Maybe. So the four of them cooked up another plot, including getting the bank manager's wife involved in a car accident to ensure that he wouldn't be around. They went through the same routine with Mr Preston as with Mrs Marrick — only they were far more brutal with him. Perhaps because he was a man. Or perhaps . . . well, I don't know. Neither of them will admit to hitting him, and they're each blaming the other. Though from witness accounts, it was definitely one of the older men who hit him, and not Jack Frobisher or Jimmy Ogden.'

'Mr Preston had a blood clot that we managed to miss,' Annabel explained. 'He never really recovered, even when he woke up for a short time.'

'The worst of it is that it looks like Jack Frobisher will escape jail, even for shooting a police officer. He has very good lawyers, and a father who is friends with most of the judges in Britain. They're playing some tune about him being a naive young man dragged down by the lower orders. They can't prove that he shot at me deliberately.'

'I'm still having trouble believing that, but obviously he did do it, sweetie.'

'He may not have money, but he has status. He may get a fine or probation, but not much more.'

'Damn him.' Annabel sighed. 'And Mummy and Daddy wanted me to marry him! In fact, they still do. Daddy phoned yesterday and muttered something about all young men having to sow wild oats. It makes me wonder what he himself got up to as a young man.'

'As long as he wasn't in Stony End with Alan Marrick eighteen years ago, you should be all right.'

'Oh, Bobbie! Don't even joke about it. Did you ever find out what the break-in was about? The one up at Mrs Marrick's?'

'It was her son firing a warning shot. It happened just before the bank robbery, remember. He thought she'd recognise his style, but Miss Hooper saw the broken lock first. He wanted to make sure his

mother kept silent after the new robbery took place. It was only when he
turned up in person that she decided
they'd been mistaken about the break-
in.'

'It's such a sad affair all around,' said
Annabel. She raised her hand, and the
engagement ring caught the sunlight
from the window. 'Yet I can't be sad.'
She smiled, looking lovelier than ever.
'Who'd have thought a few months ago
that I'd be marrying your brother?'

'It's nice to see a happy ending for
someone,' I said wistfully.

'I want you to keep the cottage,'
Annabel said, 'when I go to London.
I'm going to work at the Royal Free
Hospital. They do good things there.'

'I hate my brother,' I said with a
mock pout. 'What will I do without my
best friend?'

'I'll come and visit. And we'll all be at
Mummy and Daddy's for the wedding.'
It was going to be held on Christmas
Eve. Annabel's parents, biting back
their disappointment about Annabel's

choice of husband, had invited us all to go and stay for a week. After that, I would have to return to the cottage alone. Or maybe not.

'Do you mind if I get someone to share with me?' I asked her.

'Not at all, sweetie! I'd rather that after what happened with Carl Latimer. Have you got anyone in mind?'

'Yes, actually.'

Later that evening we went along to the village hall for Alf and Greta's wedding anniversary. We carried cakes and sandwiches, as did all the other guests — including, to my surprise, Mrs Higgins. She and Greta were great rivals for my affections and for the cookery prizes at the local fête.

'Thought I should come and pay my respects,' Mrs Higgins sniffed as she walked down the path with us. 'Anyway, they'll need some decent cake. It's been a sad time in Stony End lately.'

'Yes, it has,' I agreed, putting my arm through Mrs Higgins's. There had been too many funerals. Mrs Ogden had moved away, ashamed of her husband and son's part in the robbery. I wondered if she would try to keep up with her new neighbours. Her husband and son had insisted she knew nothing about the robbery, but I was not so sure. She liked nice things, and I suspected she did not always care how she got them. But I was sorry for her losing her son in such a dreadful way. No mother should have to go through that.

'They were good women, Mrs Marrick and Miss Hooper,' she said, 'even though we had rival stalls. By the way, the market warden has told me I can have their stall. I won't have to stand out in the cold anymore. So there's a bright side.'

As we walked into the hall, Elvis Presley's 'Love Me Tender' was playing on the record player. Alf and Greta were dancing, seemingly oblivious to everyone else. I saw Leo sitting in the corner with his brother Joe, and I waved to them. We'd been so busy we hardly had time to chat lately.

But I wasn't ready to speak to Leo yet. Across the room I saw Verity and Clyde Smith. Verity looked very pretty in a blue satin dress, and Clyde wore a suit. He looked a bit shy and uncomfortable. I also noticed that Joe was looking at them with a sullen expression. He had liked Verity for a while.

'Hello, Verity,' I said. 'Hello, Clyde.'

'Hello, WPC Blandford,' said Verity.

Clyde nodded and smiled. 'Hello.'

'Call me Bobbie, both of you. Verity, I've got a proposition to put to you. How much do you hate living in the boarding house?'

'It's a roof over my head, that's all I can say,' said Verity.

'So would you be open to moving out after Christmas? Annabel is going to live in London after her wedding, so we'll have a spare bedroom. No curfews, no silly rules or threats to chuck you out if you're a bit late getting home.'

'Really? Oh, WPC — Bobbie, that would be brilliant! And . . . and Clyde would be welcome to visit?'

'Of course! I'm glad to see you're looking well, Clyde.'

'I got some compensation,' he said. 'From the police for being beat up. I've used it to buy a car and this suit. And Mr Patel is training me to do the books so I can take over the shop one day. Me and Verity can get married in a couple of years. Mum's been crying, she's so proud.'

'As she should be, Clyde,' I said. 'I'm so sorry for all you've been through.'

'You've always been nice to me, Bobbie.'

'I hope so. Anyway, I'll leave you two to enjoy yourselves. I need to speak to Dr Stanhope. Verity, I'll be in touch about when you can move in.'

'OK. Thank you so much.'

'They look tight,' said Joe glumly when I went to sit at their table.

'There'll be someone for you one day,' I said.

'What if I don't want someone else?'

'Oh dear. Has anyone got any good news?'

'Yes, me,' said Joe, shrugging off his

fit of pique with the resilience of youth.
'We've made definite plans for my
future. I'm going to university.'

'That's great,' I said, giving Leo a
sideways glance. 'If it makes you happy,
Joe.'

'It'll make my mother happy. Anyway,
there's more,' Joe said. 'I was talking to
your brother about my prospects in the
police. He's brilliant, isn't he? He told
me that if I get a degree first, I can go to
Hendon and then straight to a senior
rank. So I can do both — finish my
education and join the police.'

'Won't your mum be upset about you
joining the police?'

'Probably. But the thing is, Mum
blames everyone for what's happened
to her except herself. The police didn't
make her go out and kill an innocent
man. Not even my father did, even if he
let her think that's what he wanted. She
made that decision. I can't live my life
the same way, Bobbie. I've got to take
responsibility, so I'm starting by deciding for myself what I'm going to do in

the future. Leo agrees — don't you, Leo?'

'Absolutely.'

'I'm glad,' I said. 'Really, Joe, it's great news.'

'Yeah, I think so.' He glanced across the room. 'I'm going to go and talk to Verity and Clyde. I don't want them thinking I'm jealous or anything. Anyway, no one else is talking to him, and that's not right.'

'He's a good kid,' I said to Leo when Joe had left us.

'Yes, he is. Of course, it's my two years of influence that got him that way,' he said with a grin.

'Oh, without a doubt.'

'It's been too long since we danced, Bobbie. Come on, let's put that right.'

We went to the dance floor just as the record changed to 'Big Girls Don't Cry' by the Four Seasons.

'And you've helped too,' Leo continued. 'I don't think I've thanked you enough for helping me with him.'

'There's no need. I'm just glad he's

doing something that makes him happy. And you . . . '

'Bobbie, it was never about the police force not being good enough for him. I told you about his mother's letters. I guess I was just trying to make everyone happy, but I ended up hurting you in the process. I'm sorry.'

I reached across and put my finger against his lips and said in a loud voice, 'I love you, Leo Stanhope.'

'I love you too.'

'No, you're not getting what I'm saying.' I was aware that some people had stopped what they were doing to listen to us. 'I love you, Leo Stanhope. I love you so much, and I didn't realise until recently how lucky I am to be able to say that in public, in front of all our friends and family. I know I get anxious about the way things are going with us, but I realise now how very easy it is to love you and to be loved in return. We don't have to hide away in shame and pretend to be something we're not. No one can ever use our love for each other against us. So I want you and everyone else to know that I love you and I always will.'

There was a chorus of 'awww's around the room. I started to blush, realising that I was stealing Alf and Greta's thunder. 'Sorry,' I mouthed to them, but they both laughed.

'That's the most wonderful thing anyone has ever said to me,' Leo said, pulling me close. 'Did I ever tell you how stupidly grateful I am that you're mine?'

'Really? Because that's how I feel about you. All the time. I don't deserve you.'

'No, you deserve much better. And you don't have to be grateful for something that's so easy for me. Loving you is the best thing I've ever done. But can this not be our song?'

'I love this song.'

'It's good, but it's not about us. We have no need to shed tears for each other, Bobbie.'

I put my head on his shoulder as a

quieter song started. Big girls didn't cry. But if she was very happy, a secret tear might fall onto the shoulder of the man she loved.

We do hope that you have enjoyed reading this large print book.

Did you know that all of our titles are available for purchase?

We publish a wide range of high quality large print books including:
Romances, Mysteries, Classics
General Fiction
Non Fiction and Westerns

Special interest titles available in large print are:
The Little Oxford Dictionary
Music Book, Song Book
Hymn Book, Service Book

Also available from us courtesy of Oxford University Press:
Young Readers' Dictionary
(large print edition)
Young Readers' Thesaurus
(large print edition)

For further information or a free brochure, please contact us at:
Ulverscroft Large Print Books Ltd.,
The Green, Bradgate Road, Anstey,
Leicester, LE7 7FU, England.
Tel: (00 44) **0116 236 4325**
Fax: (00 44) **0116 234 0205**

Other titles in the
Linford Romance Library:

THE DARK MARSHES

Sally Quilford

England, late 1800s: Henrietta Marsh
has felt a shadow following her for
most of her life. There are whispers
among her colleagues that this darkness led to the violent death of her
parents. When she is incarcerated
in a mental hospital, she charts the
events that led her there. Meanwhile, her only friend, and the man
she loves, fight to save her. But can
Henrietta be trusted, or is she truly
mad — and guilty of the heinous
crimes of which she is suspected?

BOUND BY A COMMON ENEMY

Lucy Oliver

Tied to the violent Edmund by a betrothal contract, Elizabeth Farrell gains an unexpected opportunity for deliverance when their bridal party is stopped in the forest by a band of men. William Downes offers to pay off her contract — if she will enter a temporary marriage of convenience with him instead. Scarred by his past, William refuses to consider marrying for love, but needs a bride to protect both his sister's illegitimate child and the family's land. Will Elizabeth accept the bargain?

TIME FOR CHANGE

Chrissie Loveday

1977: William Cobridge has sold the factory and taken early retirement, but his wife Paula can't help but feel that something is still missing from her life. She wants to move to a smaller, more modern house, but knows that Nellie, her mother-in-law, will never accept the change. In fact, Nellie isn't really coping with anything at the moment . . . Meanwhile, William and Paula's daughter Sophie is sharing a flat with her Aunt Bella, who is exasperating both as her flatmate and boss at work — and Sophie wants out . . .

A SMOKY MOUNTAIN CHRISTMAS

Angela Britnell

Gill Robinson's fiancé has called off their Christmas Eve wedding, and she's dreading the upcoming holidays. Out of the blue, she has the chance to escape: her Aunt Betsy has a small B&B in the Smoky Mountains and needs a break, so Gill flies out to help. But when she meets handsome, enigmatic Luke Sawyer, she knows the quiet time she'd envisioned isn't going to happen. Ostensibly the inn's handyman, Gill suspects there's a lot more to Luke than he's letting on . . .

ORKNEY MYSTERY

Miranda Barnes

When Emma Mason inherits a house on Orkney from her Great-aunt Freda, she is mystified — she knows nothing about Freda, and her parents are of little help. The only thing for it is to visit Orkney herself. On the ferry, she meets Gregor McEwan, a wildlife photographer and passionate Orcadian. Together they begin to piece together Freda's story, whilst becoming increasingly attracted to each other — though there are serious obstacles in their way: Gregor is struggling with a past tragedy, and Emma's life is firmly rooted in Tyneside . . .